visit us at
www.abdopublishing.com

Published by Magic Wagon, a division of the ABDO Publishing Group, 8000 West 78th Street, Edina, Minnesota 55439. Copyright © 2009 by Abdo Consulting Group, Inc. International copyrights reserved in all countries. All rights reserved. No part of this book may be reproduced in any form without written permission from the publisher.
Graphic Planet™ is a trademark and logo of MagicWagon.

Printed in the United States of America, North Mankato, Minnesota.

Adapted by Joeming Dunn
Illustrated by Rod Espinosa
Edited by Stephanie Hedlund and Rochelle Baltzer
Interior layout and design by Antarctic Press
Cover art by Rod Espinosa
Cover design by Neil Klinepier

Library of Congress Cataloging-in-Publication Data

Dunn, Joeming W.
    William Shakespeare's Romeo and Juliet / adapted by Joeming Dunn; illustrated by Rod Espinosa.
        p. cm. -- (Graphic Shakespeare)
    Summary: Retells, in comic book format, Shakespeare's play of the tragic consequences of a deadly feud between two rival families in Renaissance Verona.
    ISBN 978-1-60270-193-9
    1. Graphic novels. [1. Graphic novels. 2. Shakespeare, William, 1564-1616--Adaptations.] I. Espinosa, Rod, ill. II. Shakespeare, William, 1564-1616. Romeo and Juliet. III. Title. IV. Title: Romeo and Juliet.

PZ7.7.D86Wi 2008
741.5'973--dc22

                                                                                2008010744

012009
022010

Table of Contents

Cast of Characters

Capulet
Lord of a ruling house

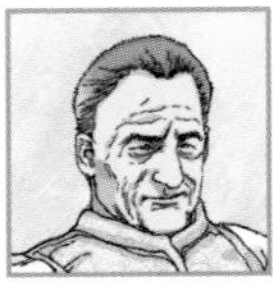

Gregory
Capulet servant

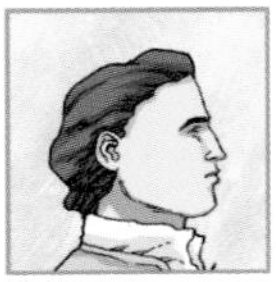

Juliet
Capulet's only daughter

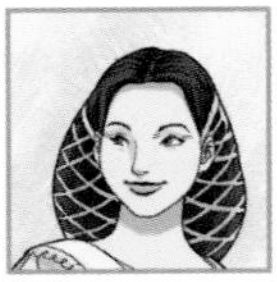

Lady Capulet
Capulet's wife

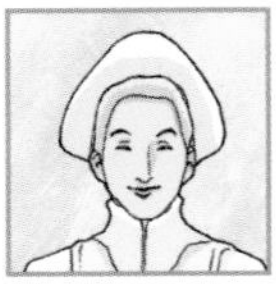

Nurse
Capulet servant

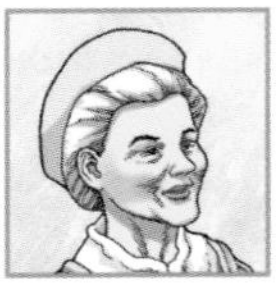

Sampson
Capulet servant

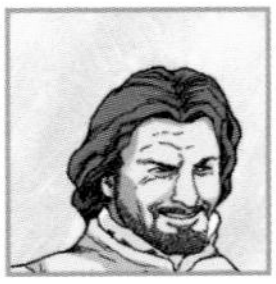

Tybalt
Capulet's nephew

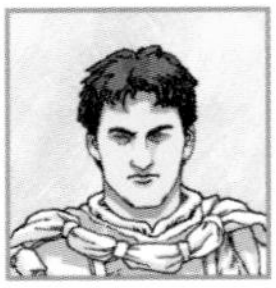

Paris
Juliet's suitor

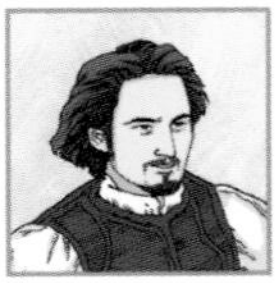

Abraham
Montague servant

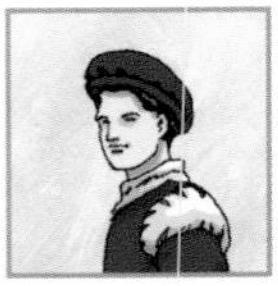

Balthasar
Montague servant

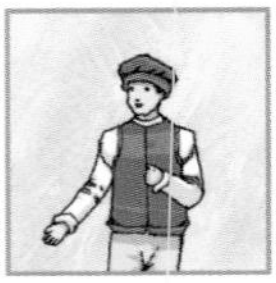

Benvolio
Montague's nephew

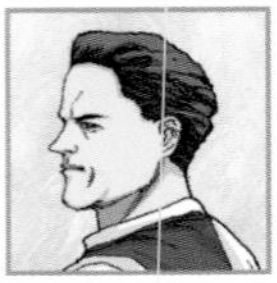

Lady Montague
Montague's wife

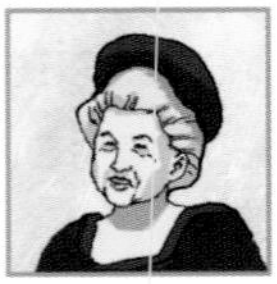

Mercutio
Romeo's friend

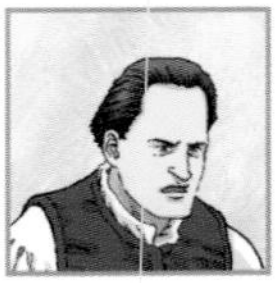

Montague
Lord of a ruling house

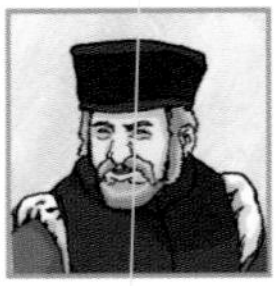

Romeo
Montague's only son

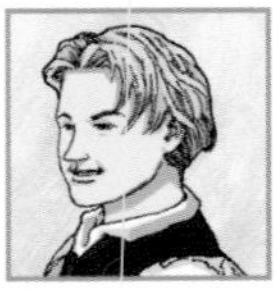

Friar Laurence

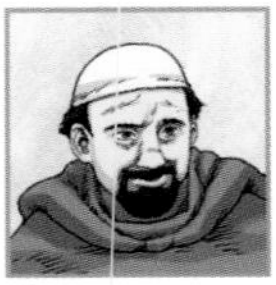

Prince Escalus of Verona

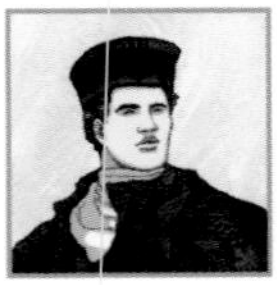

Our Setting

Though Shakespeare never visited Italy, *Romeo and Juliet* is set in Verona, the capital of the Veneto province in Italy. Verona was founded in ancient times. It became a Roman city in 89 BC. It was later occupied by many of its neighboring rulers.

After 1260 AD, Verona became more settled under the della Scala family. It is believed Shakespeare set *Romeo and Juliet* in the 1300s or 1400s, when Bartolomeo della Scala ruled the city. This tradition was set by the original Italian tale by Matteo Bandello.

Verona contains the richest collection of Roman architecture, Greek and Roman artifacts, and medieval painting. Today, the city also contains several sites made famous by *Romeo and Juliet* including Juliet's balcony and the Tomb of Juliet.

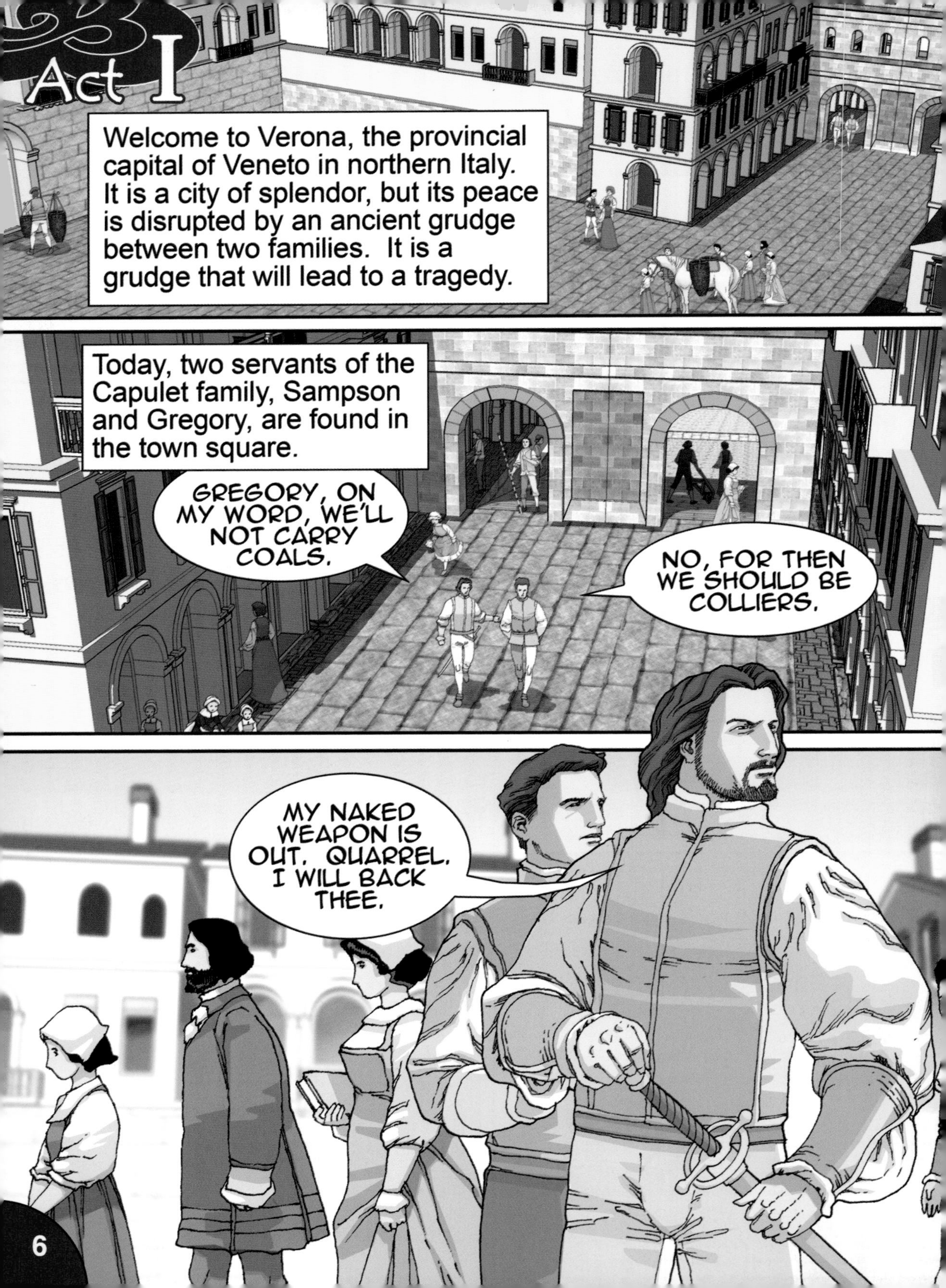
Act I
Welcome to Verona, the provincial capital of Veneto in northern Italy. It is a city of splendor, but its peace is disrupted by an ancient grudge between two families. It is a grudge that will lead to a tragedy.
Today, two servants of the Capulet family, Sampson and Gregory, are found in the town square.
GREGORY, ON MY WORD, WE'LL NOT CARRY COALS.
NO, FOR THEN WE SHOULD BE COLLIERS.
MY NAKED WEAPON IS OUT. QUARREL, I WILL BACK THEE.

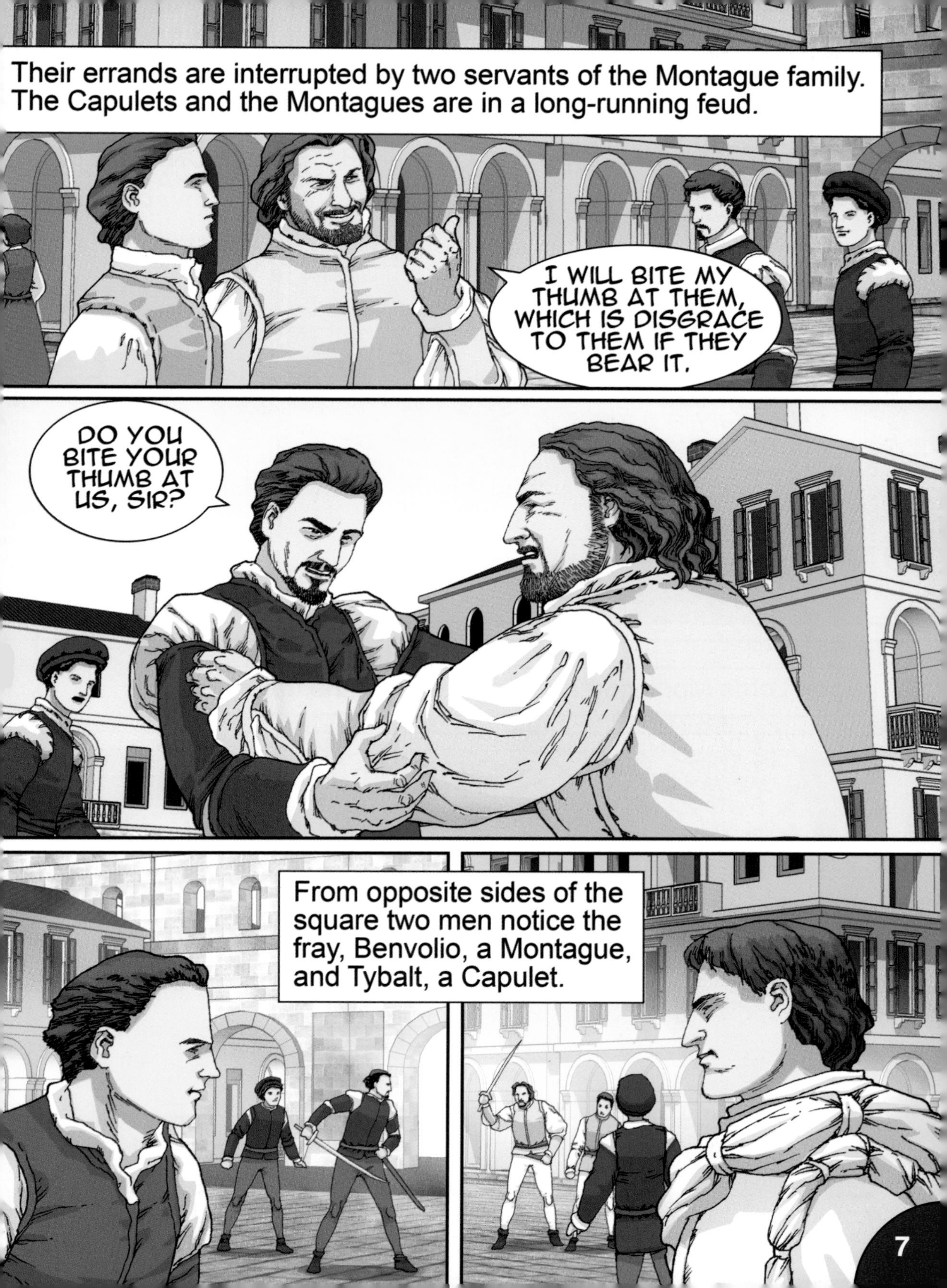
Their errands are interrupted by two servants of the Montague family. The Capulets and the Montagues are in a long-running feud.
I WILL BITE MY THUMB AT THEM, WHICH IS DISGRACE TO THEM IF THEY BEAR IT.
DO YOU BITE YOUR THUMB AT US, SIR?
From opposite sides of the square two men notice the fray, Benvolio, a Montague, and Tybalt, a Capulet.

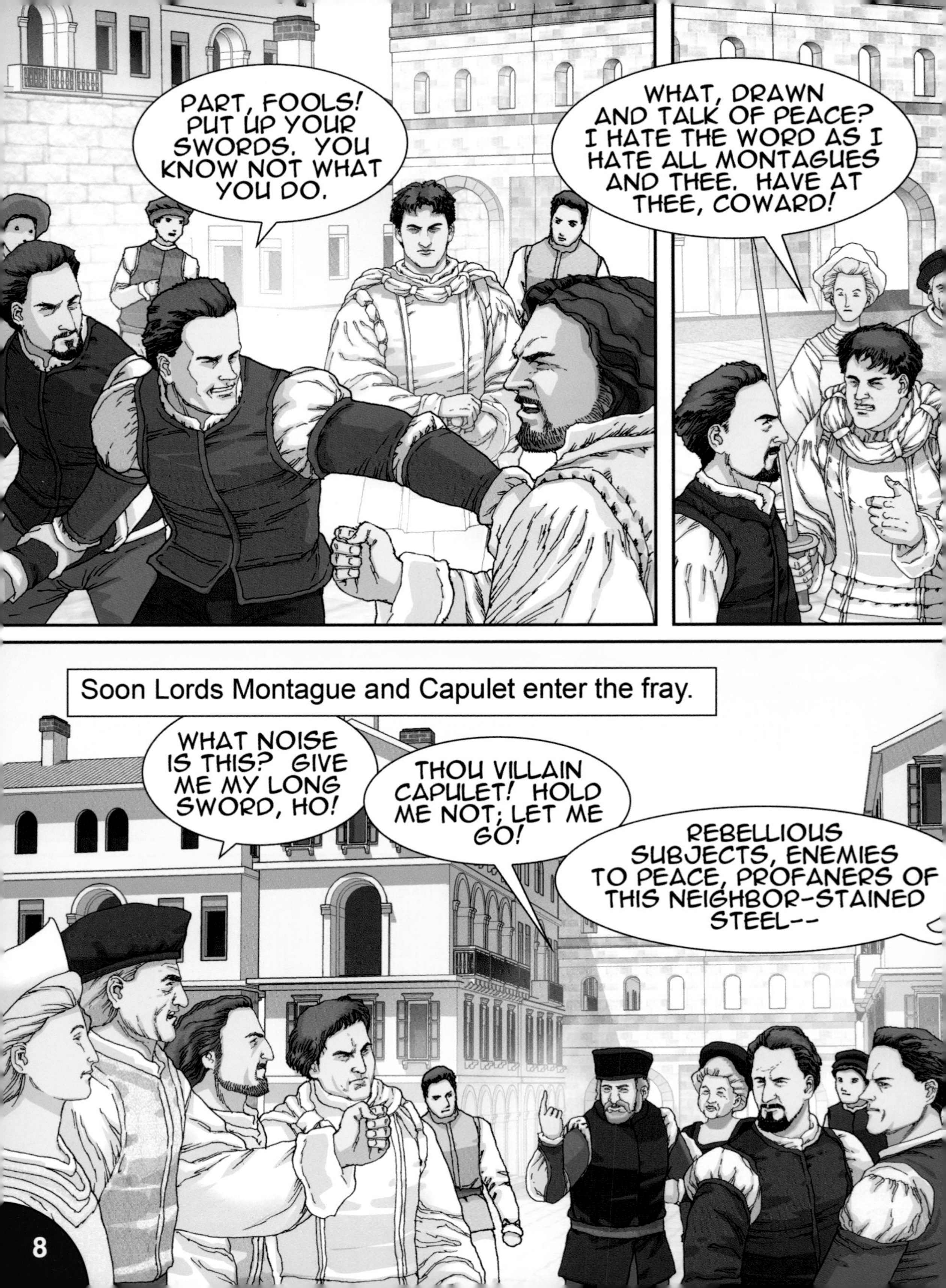
PART, FOOLS! PUT UP YOUR SWORDS. YOU KNOW NOT WHAT YOU DO.
WHAT, DRAWN AND TALK OF PEACE? I HATE THE WORD AS I HATE ALL MONTAGUES AND THEE. HAVE AT THEE, COWARD!
Soon Lords Montague and Capulet enter the fray.
WHAT NOISE IS THIS? GIVE ME MY LONG SWORD, HO!
THOU VILLAIN CAPULET! HOLD ME NOT; LET ME GO!
REBELLIOUS SUBJECTS, ENEMIES TO PEACE, PROFANERS OF THIS NEIGHBOR-STAINED STEEL--

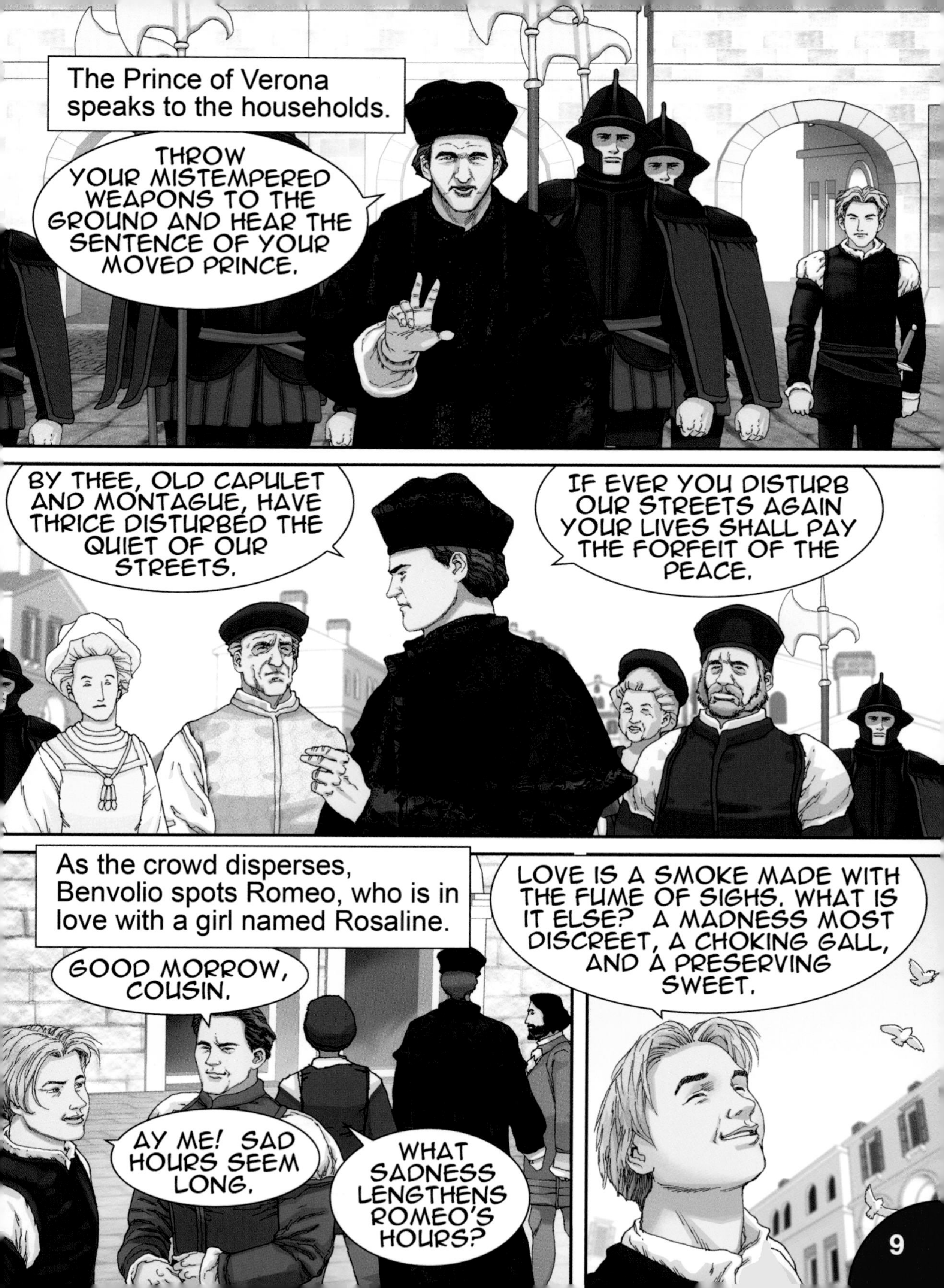
The Prince of Verona speaks to the households.
THROW YOUR MISTEMPERED WEAPONS TO THE GROUND AND HEAR THE SENTENCE OF YOUR MOVED PRINCE.
BY THEE, OLD CAPULET AND MONTAGUE, HAVE THRICE DISTURBED THE QUIET OF OUR STREETS.
IF EVER YOU DISTURB OUR STREETS AGAIN YOUR LIVES SHALL PAY THE FORFEIT OF THE PEACE.
As the crowd disperses, Benvolio spots Romeo, who is in love with a girl named Rosaline.
GOOD MORROW, COUSIN.
AY ME! SAD HOURS SEEM LONG.
WHAT SADNESS LENGTHENS ROMEO'S HOURS?
LOVE IS A SMOKE MADE WITH THE FUME OF SIGHS. WHAT IS IT ELSE? A MADNESS MOST DISCREET, A CHOKING GALL, AND A PRESERVING SWEET.

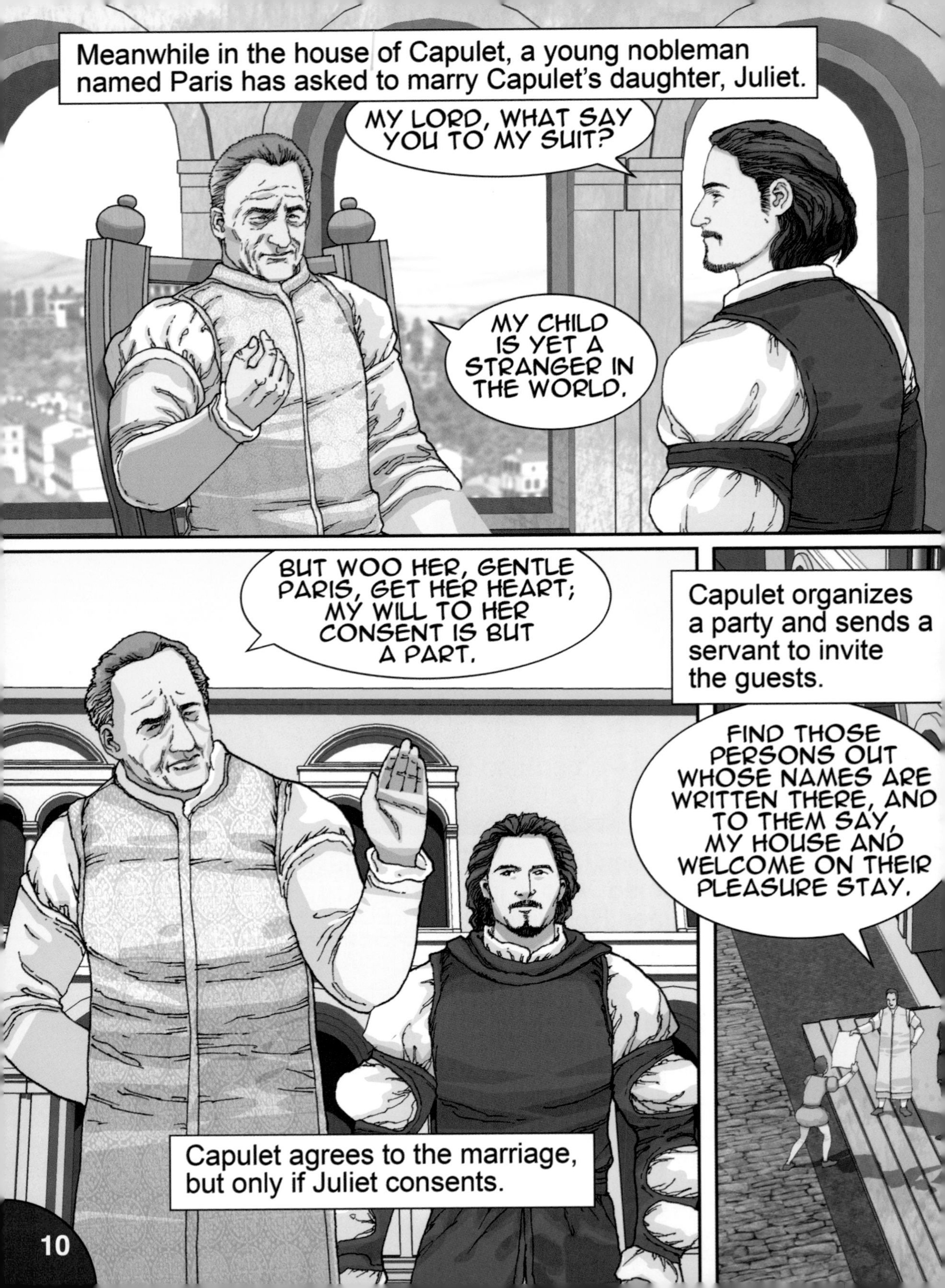

Meanwhile in the house of Capulet, a young nobleman named Paris has asked to marry Capulet's daughter, Juliet.
MY LORD, WHAT SAY YOU TO MY SUIT?
MY CHILD IS YET A STRANGER IN THE WORLD.
BUT WOO HER, GENTLE PARIS, GET HER HEART; MY WILL TO HER CONSENT IS BUT A PART.
Capulet agrees to the marriage, but only if Juliet consents.
Capulet organizes a party and sends a servant to invite the guests.
FIND THOSE PERSONS OUT WHOSE NAMES ARE WRITTEN THERE, AND TO THEM SAY, MY HOUSE AND WELCOME ON THEIR PLEASURE STAY.

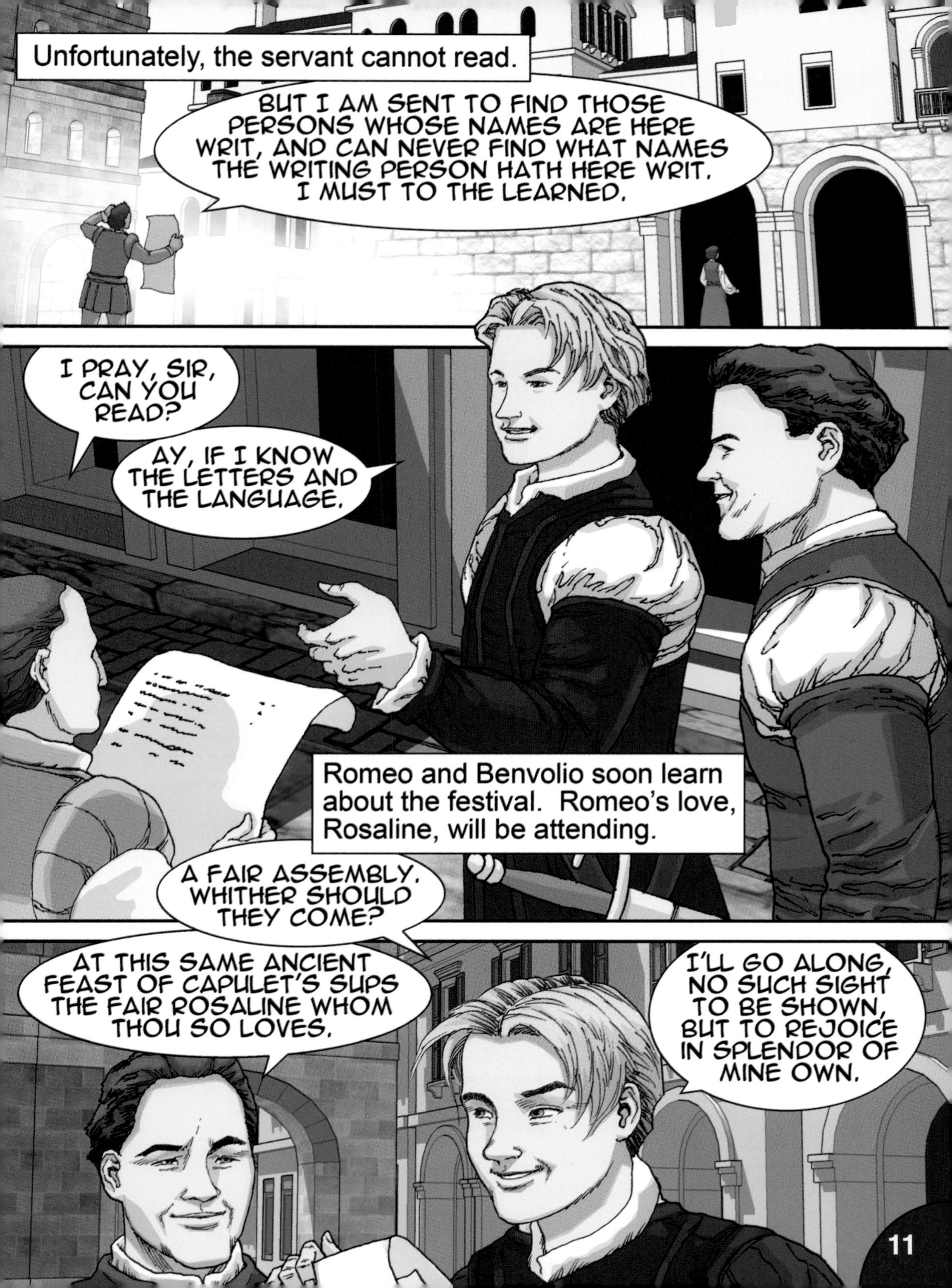

Unfortunately, the servant cannot read.
BUT I AM SENT TO FIND THOSE PERSONS WHOSE NAMES ARE HERE WRIT, AND CAN NEVER FIND WHAT NAMES THE WRITING PERSON HATH HERE WRIT. I MUST TO THE LEARNED.
I PRAY, SIR, CAN YOU READ?
AY, IF I KNOW THE LETTERS AND THE LANGUAGE.
Romeo and Benvolio soon learn about the festival. Romeo's love, Rosaline, will be attending.
A FAIR ASSEMBLY. WHITHER SHOULD THEY COME?
AT THIS SAME ANCIENT FEAST OF CAPULET'S SUPS THE FAIR ROSALINE WHOM THOU SO LOVES.
I'LL GO ALONG, NO SUCH SIGHT TO BE SHOWN, BUT TO REJOICE IN SPLENDOR OF MINE OWN.

At the Capulet's, Juliet and her mother discuss Paris.

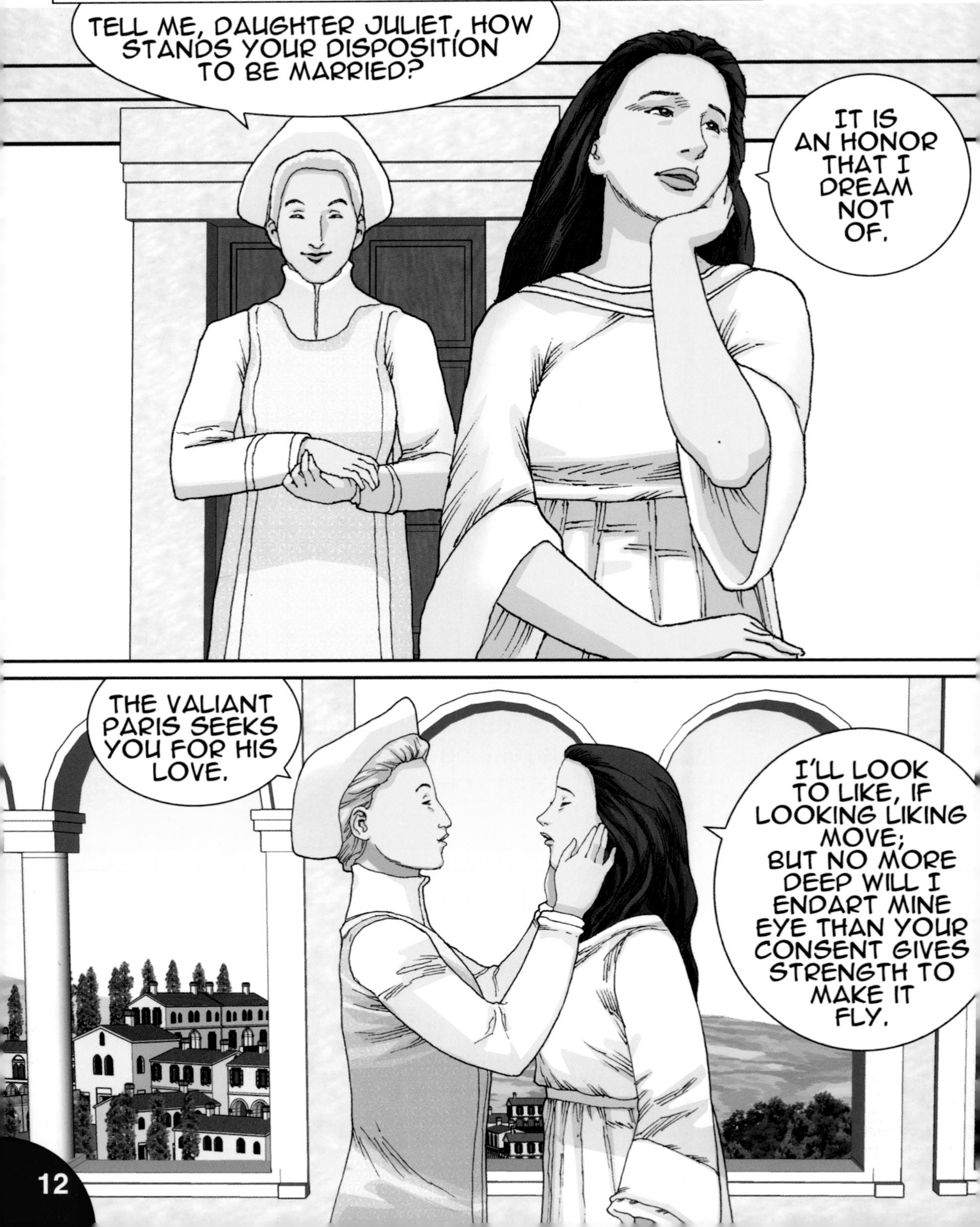

TELL ME, DAUGHTER JULIET, HOW STANDS YOUR DISPOSITION TO BE MARRIED?
IT IS AN HONOR THAT I DREAM NOT OF.
THE VALIANT PARIS SEEKS YOU FOR HIS LOVE.
I'LL LOOK TO LIKE, IF LOOKING LIKING MOVE; BUT NO MORE DEEP WILL I ENDART MINE EYE THAN YOUR CONSENT GIVES STRENGTH TO MAKE IT FLY.

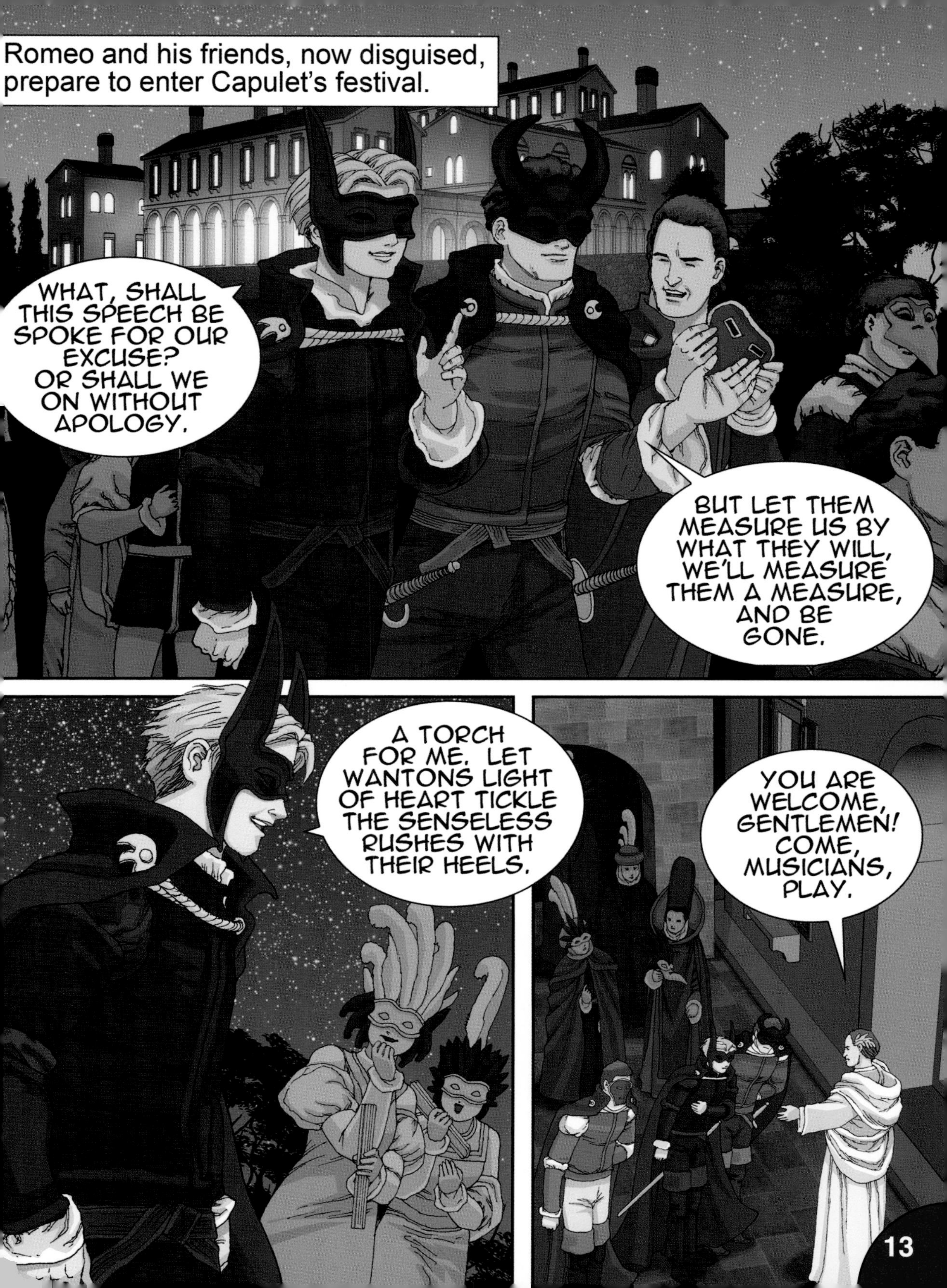
Romeo and his friends, now disguised, prepare to enter Capulet's festival.
WHAT, SHALL THIS SPEECH BE SPOKE FOR OUR EXCUSE? OR SHALL WE ON WITHOUT APOLOGY.
BUT LET THEM MEASURE US BY WHAT THEY WILL, WE'LL MEASURE THEM A MEASURE, AND BE GONE.
A TORCH FOR ME. LET WANTONS LIGHT OF HEART TICKLE THE SENSELESS RUSHES WITH THEIR HEELS.
YOU ARE WELCOME, GENTLEMEN! COME, MUSICIANS, PLAY.

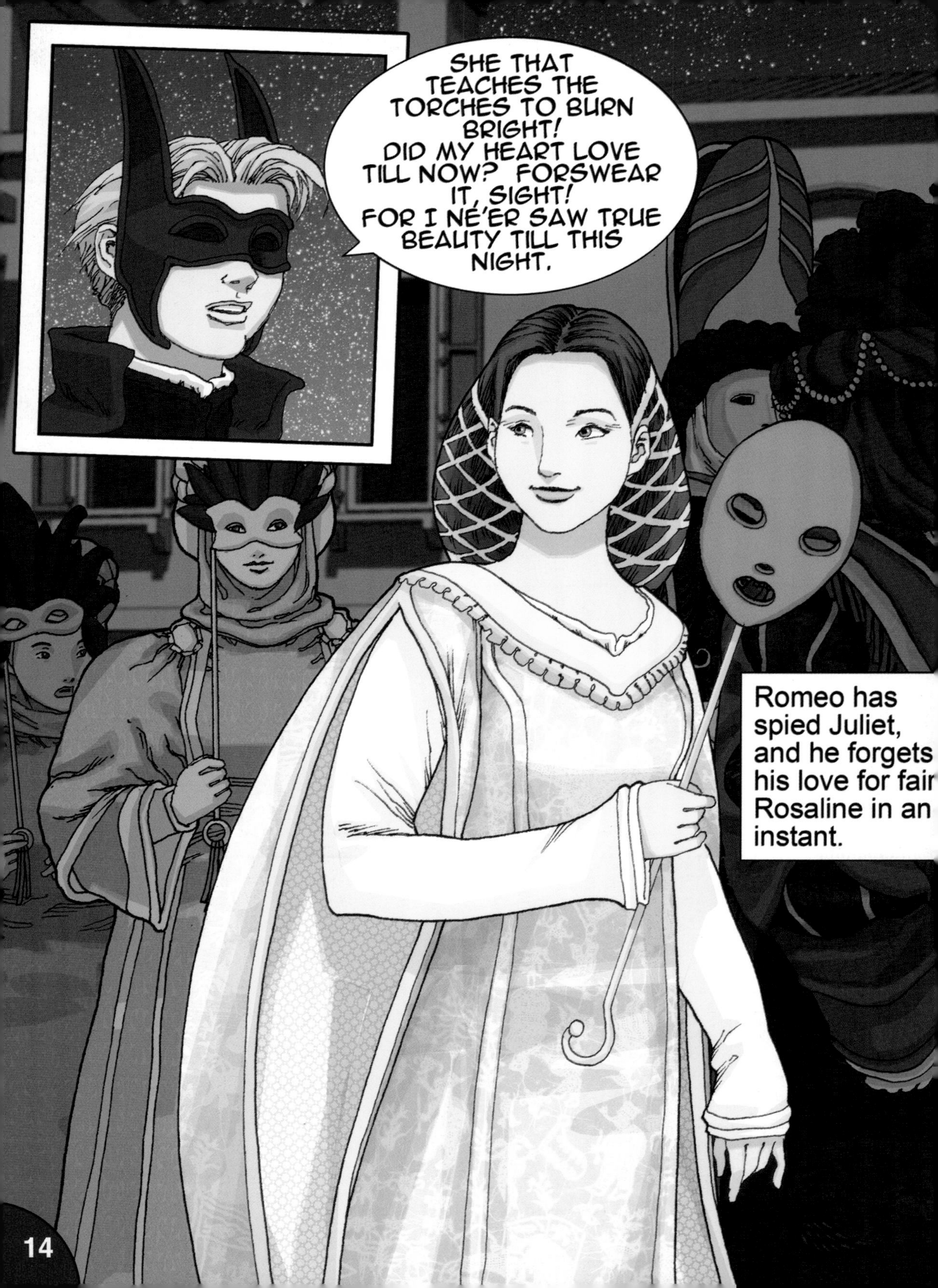
SHE THAT TEACHES THE TORCHES TO BURN BRIGHT! DID MY HEART LOVE TILL NOW? FORSWEAR IT, SIGHT! FOR I NE'ER SAW TRUE BEAUTY TILL THIS NIGHT.
Romeo has spied Juliet, and he forgets his love for fair Rosaline in an instant.

Tybalt is near and unmasks Romeo!

THIS, BY HIS VOICE, SHOULD BE A MONTAGUE.

UNCLE, THIS IS A MONTAGUE, OUR FOE, A VILLAIN THAT IS HITHER COME IN SPITE TO SCORN AT OUR SOLEMNITY THIS NIGHT.

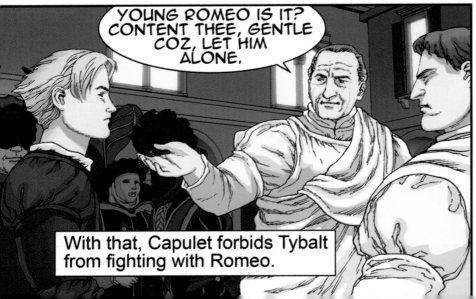

YOUNG ROMEO IS IT? CONTENT THEE, GENTLE COZ, LET HIM ALONE.

IT FITS WHEN SUCH A VILLAIN IS A GUEST. I'LL NOT ENDURE HIM.

With that, Capulet forbids Tybalt from fighting with Romeo.

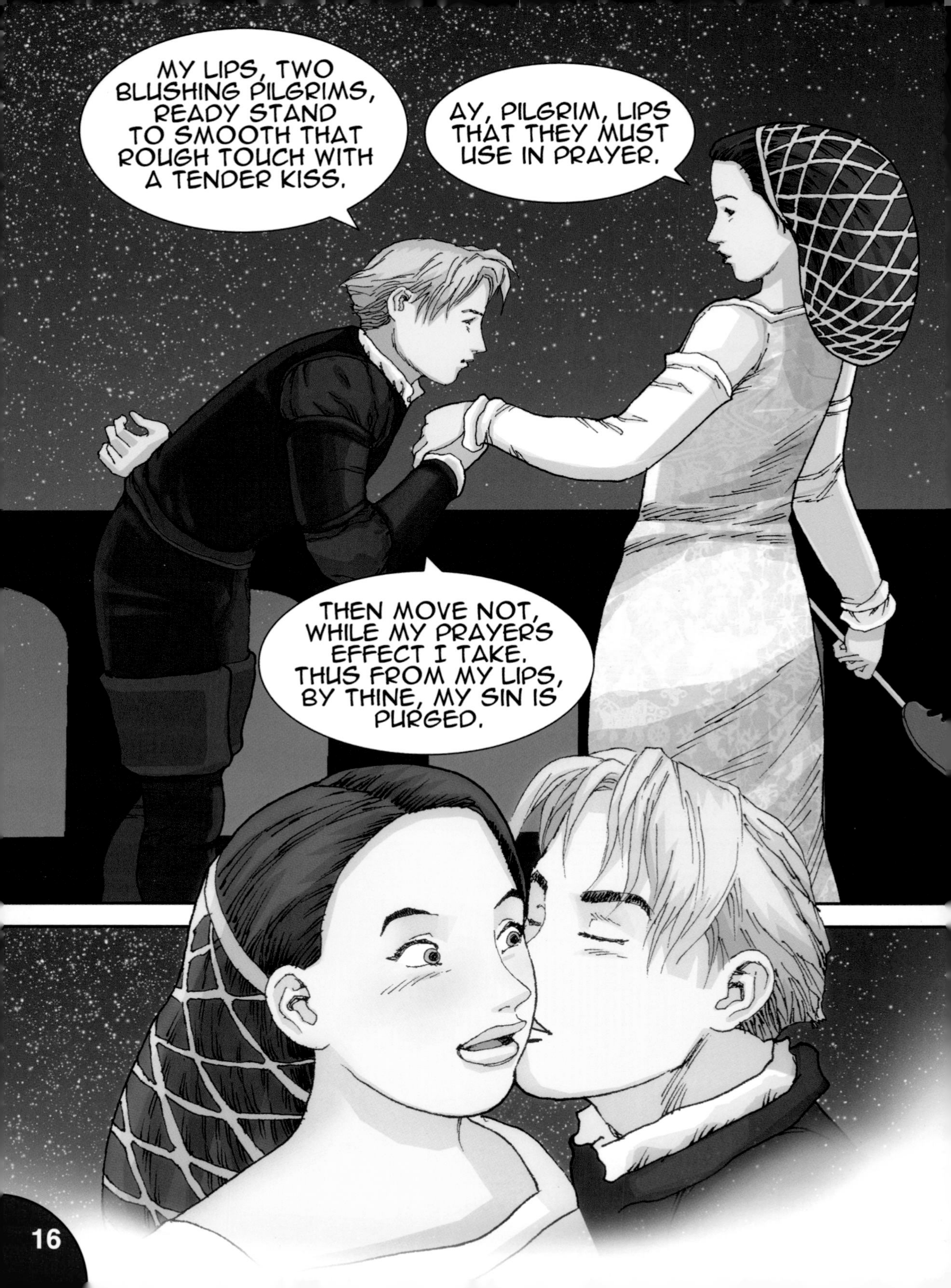
MY LIPS, TWO BLUSHING PILGRIMS, READY STAND TO SMOOTH THAT ROUGH TOUCH WITH A TENDER KISS.
AY, PILGRIM, LIPS THAT THEY MUST USE IN PRAYER.
THEN MOVE NOT, WHILE MY PRAYER'S EFFECT I TAKE. THUS FROM MY LIPS, BY THINE, MY SIN IS PURGED.

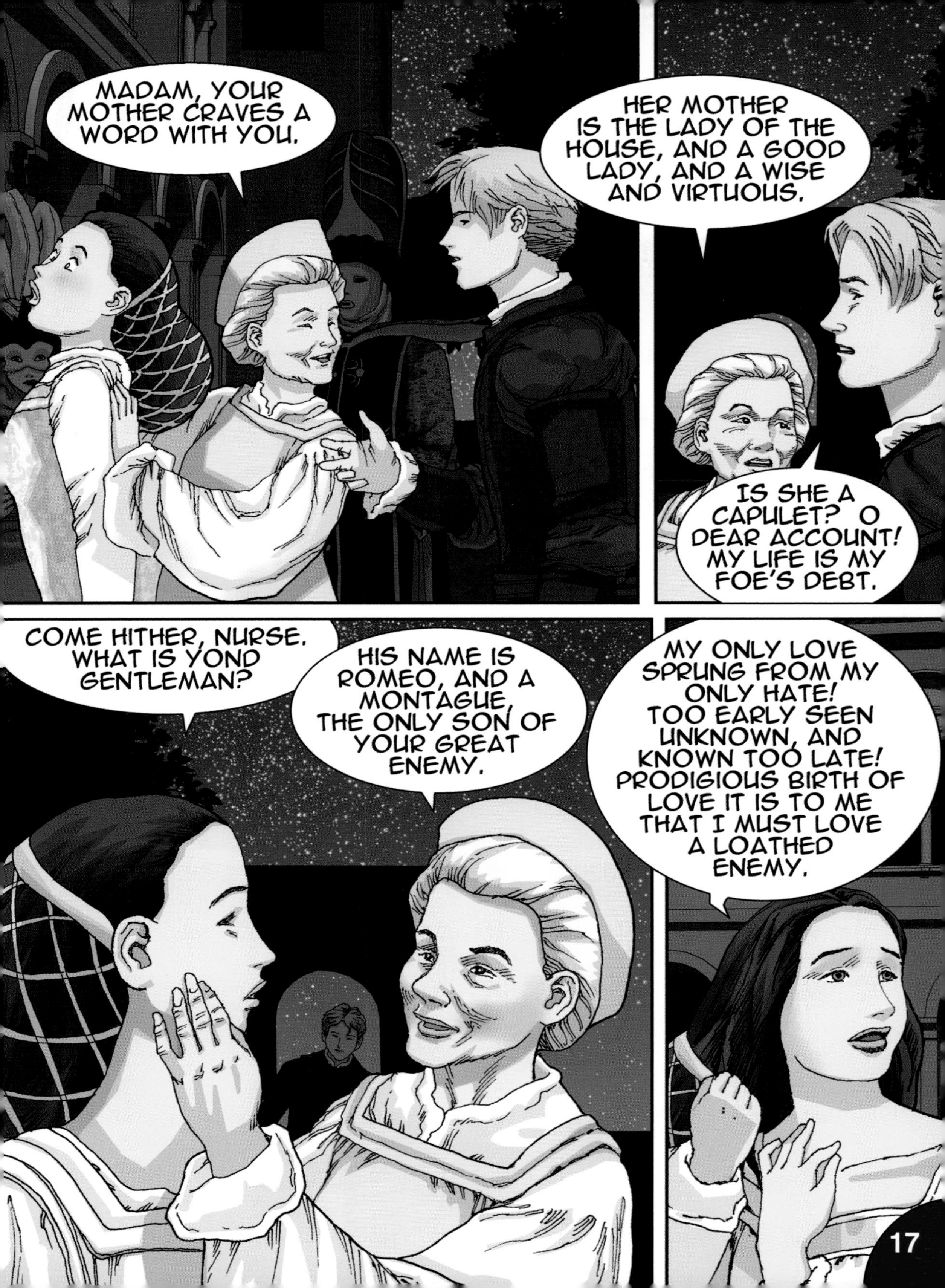
MADAM, YOUR MOTHER CRAVES A WORD WITH YOU.
HER MOTHER IS THE LADY OF THE HOUSE, AND A GOOD LADY, AND A WISE AND VIRTUOUS.
IS SHE A CAPULET? O DEAR ACCOUNT! MY LIFE IS MY FOE'S DEBT.
COME HITHER, NURSE. WHAT IS YOND GENTLEMAN?
HIS NAME IS ROMEO, AND A MONTAGUE, THE ONLY SON OF YOUR GREAT ENEMY.
MY ONLY LOVE SPRUNG FROM MY ONLY HATE! TOO EARLY SEEN UNKNOWN, AND KNOWN TOO LATE! PRODIGIOUS BIRTH OF LOVE IT IS TO ME THAT I MUST LOVE A LOATHED ENEMY.

Act II

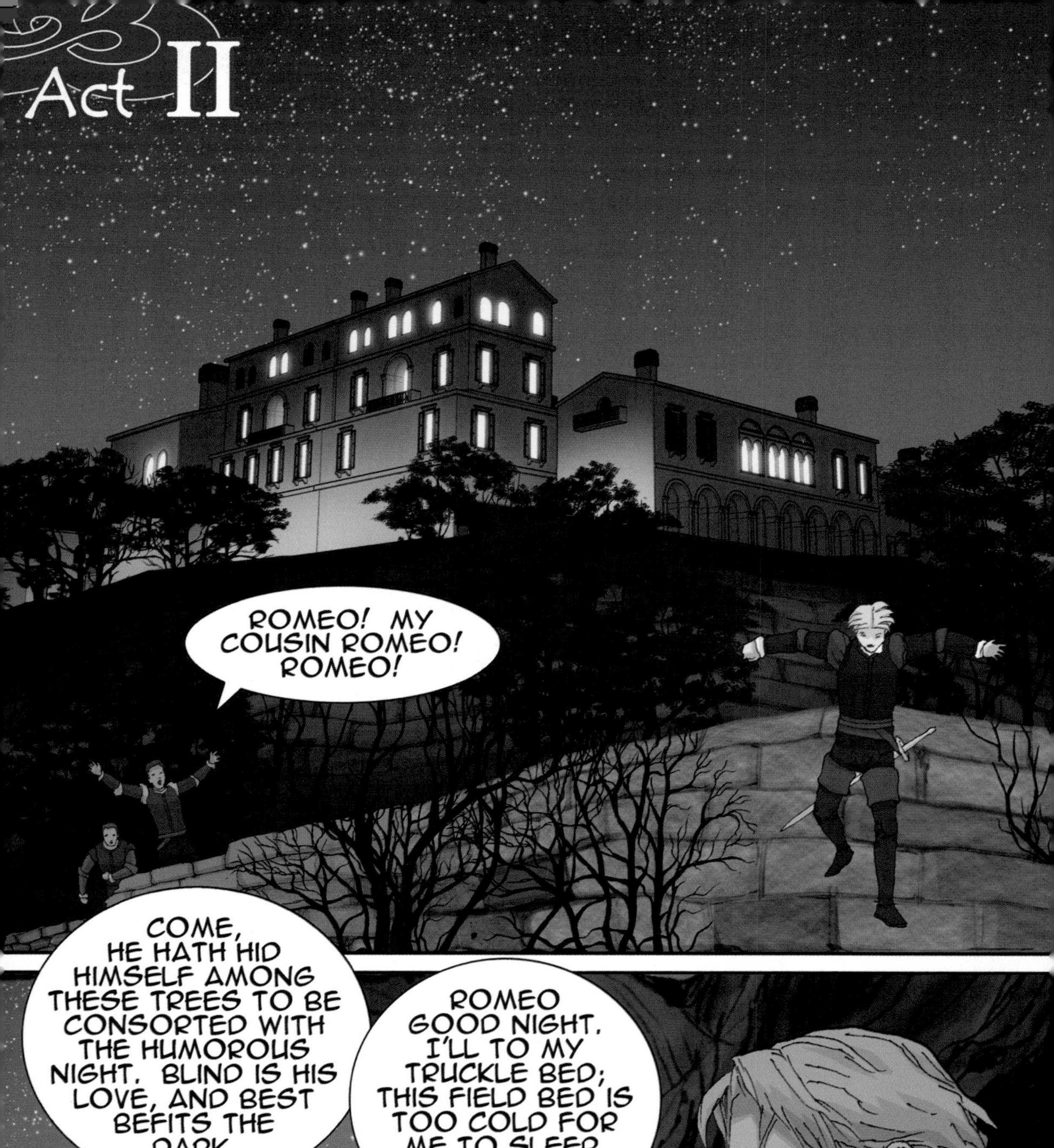
ROMEO! MY COUSIN ROMEO! ROMEO!

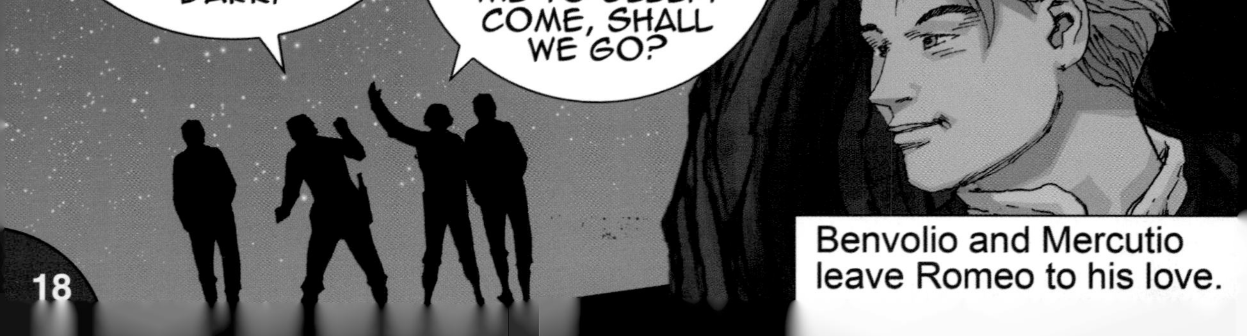
COME, HE HATH HID HIMSELF AMONG THESE TREES TO BE CONSORTED WITH THE HUMOROUS NIGHT. BLIND IS HIS LOVE, AND BEST BEFITS THE DARK.
ROMEO GOOD NIGHT. I'LL TO MY TRUCKLE BED; THIS FIELD BED IS TOO COLD FOR ME TO SLEEP. COME, SHALL WE GO?
Benvolio and Mercutio leave Romeo to his love.

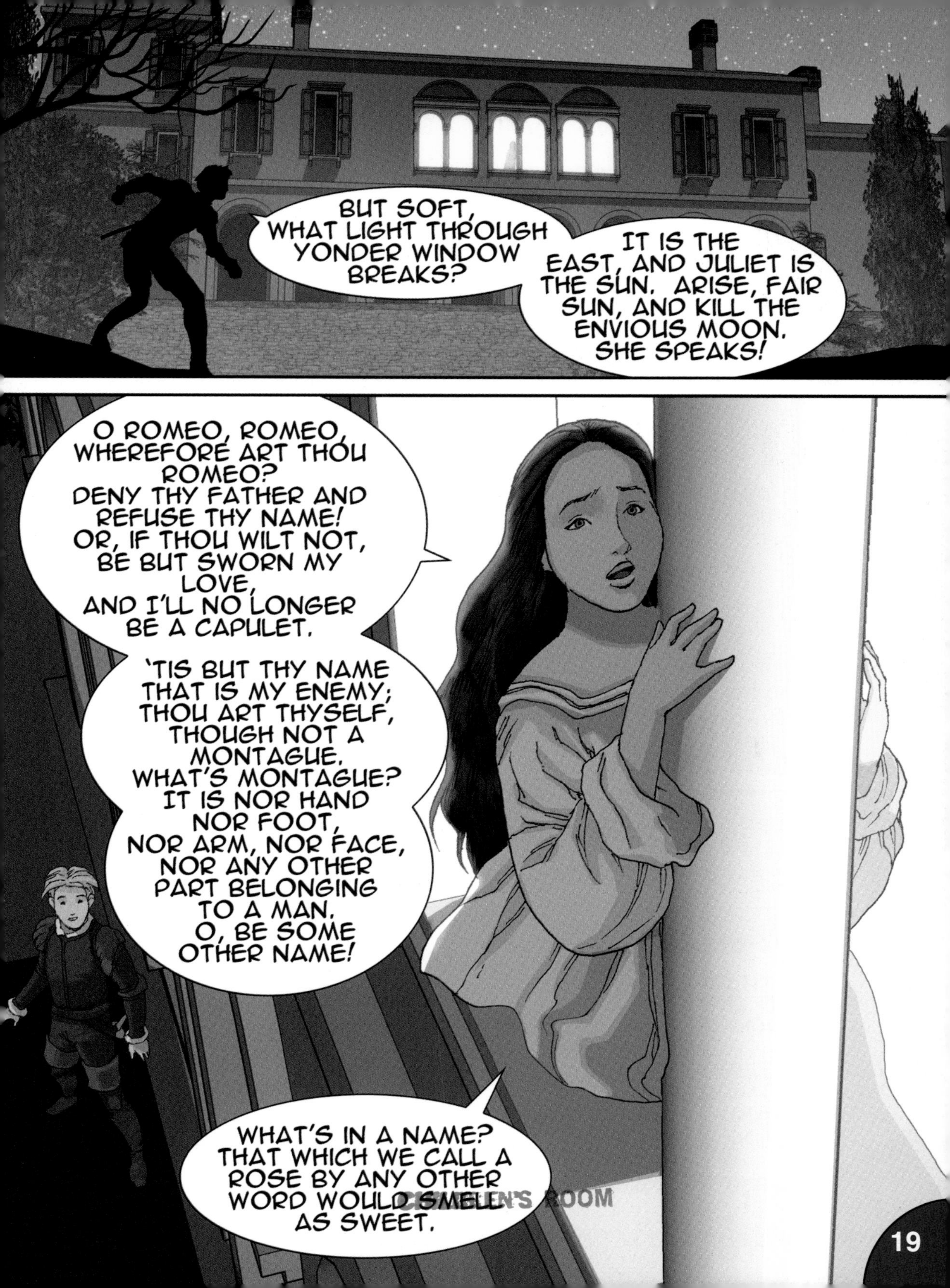
BUT SOFT, WHAT LIGHT THROUGH YONDER WINDOW BREAKS?
IT IS THE EAST, AND JULIET IS THE SUN. ARISE, FAIR SUN, AND KILL THE ENVIOUS MOON. SHE SPEAKS!
O ROMEO, ROMEO, WHEREFORE ART THOU ROMEO? DENY THY FATHER AND REFUSE THY NAME! OR, IF THOU WILT NOT, BE BUT SWORN MY LOVE, AND I'LL NO LONGER BE A CAPULET.
'TIS BUT THY NAME THAT IS MY ENEMY; THOU ART THYSELF, THOUGH NOT A MONTAGUE. WHAT'S MONTAGUE? IT IS NOR HAND NOR FOOT, NOR ARM, NOR FACE, NOR ANY OTHER PART BELONGING TO A MAN. O, BE SOME OTHER NAME!
WHAT'S IN A NAME? THAT WHICH WE CALL A ROSE BY ANY OTHER WORD WOULD SMELL AS SWEET.

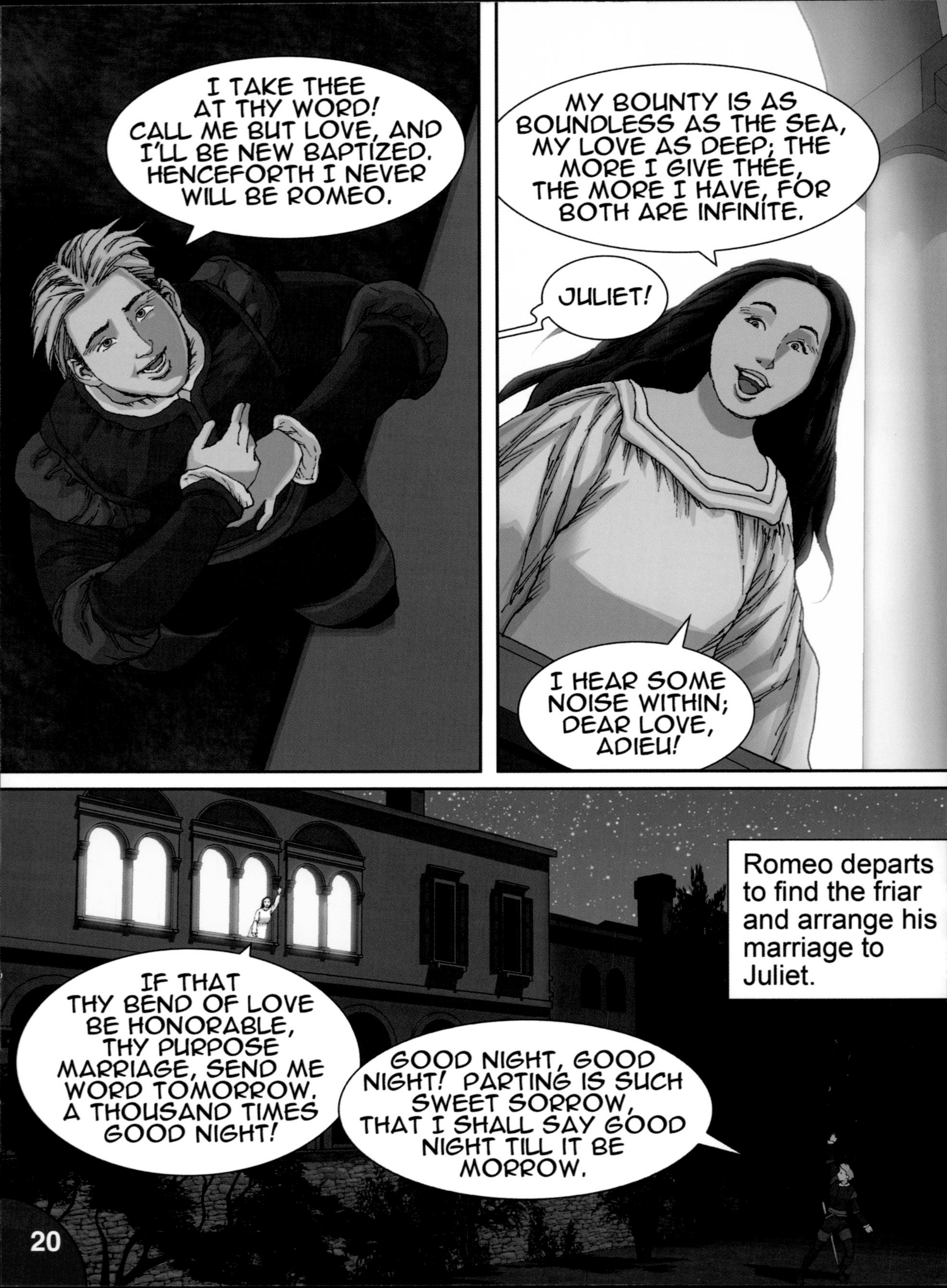
I TAKE THEE AT THY WORD! CALL ME BUT LOVE, AND I'LL BE NEW BAPTIZED. HENCEFORTH I NEVER WILL BE ROMEO.
MY BOUNTY IS AS BOUNDLESS AS THE SEA, MY LOVE AS DEEP; THE MORE I GIVE THEE, THE MORE I HAVE, FOR BOTH ARE INFINITE.
JULIET!
I HEAR SOME NOISE WITHIN; DEAR LOVE, ADIEU!
Romeo departs to find the friar and arrange his marriage to Juliet.
IF THAT THY BEND OF LOVE BE HONORABLE, THY PURPOSE MARRIAGE, SEND ME WORD TOMORROW. A THOUSAND TIMES GOOD NIGHT!
GOOD NIGHT, GOOD NIGHT! PARTING IS SUCH SWEET SORROW, THAT I SHALL SAY GOOD NIGHT TILL IT BE MORROW.

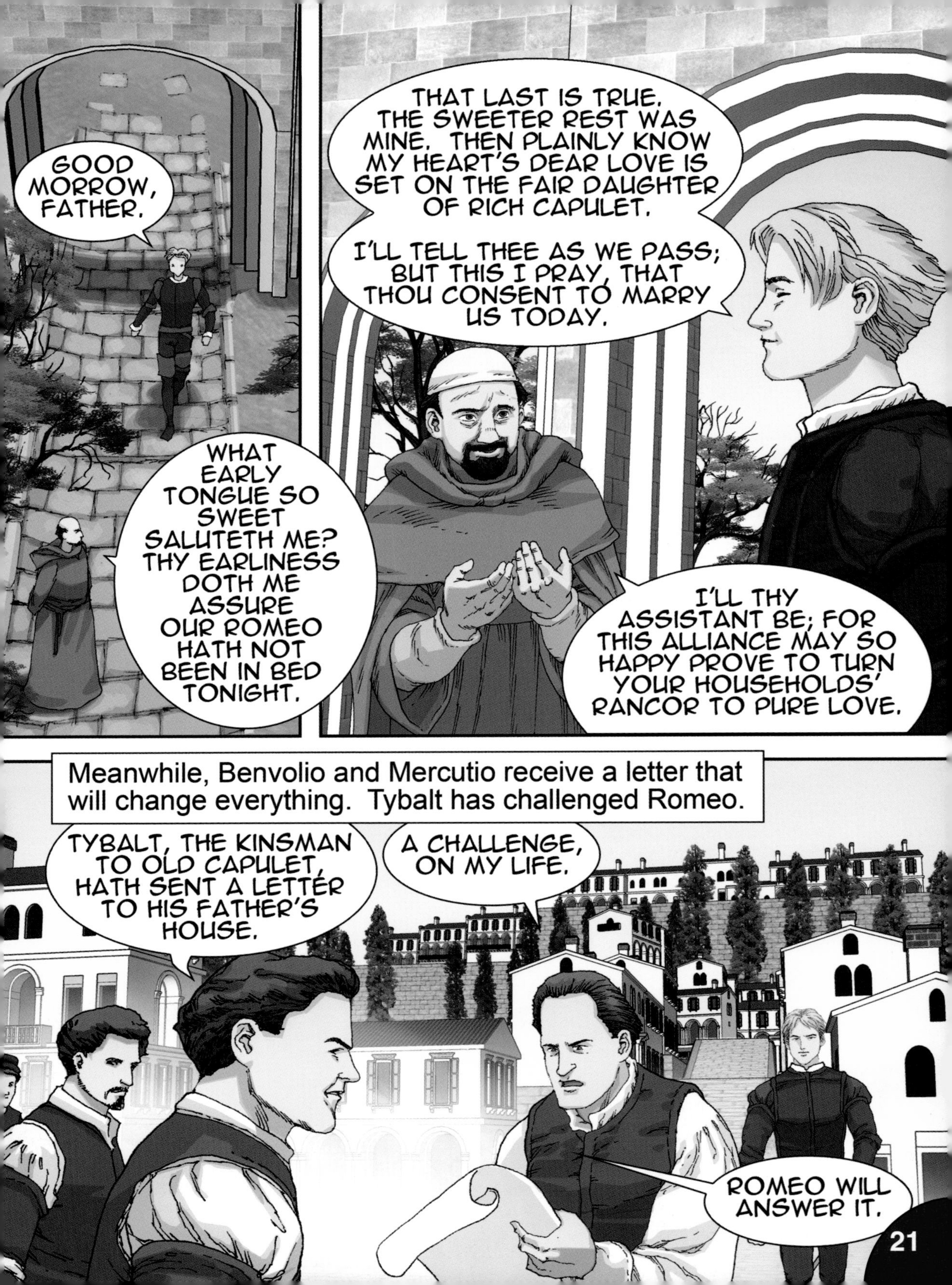
GOOD MORROW, FATHER.
WHAT EARLY TONGUE SO SWEET SALUTETH ME? THY EARLINESS DOTH ME ASSURE OUR ROMEO HATH NOT BEEN IN BED TONIGHT.
THAT LAST IS TRUE. THE SWEETER REST WAS MINE. THEN PLAINLY KNOW MY HEART'S DEAR LOVE IS SET ON THE FAIR DAUGHTER OF RICH CAPULET.
I'LL TELL THEE AS WE PASS; BUT THIS I PRAY, THAT THOU CONSENT TO MARRY US TODAY.
I'LL THY ASSISTANT BE; FOR THIS ALLIANCE MAY SO HAPPY PROVE TO TURN YOUR HOUSEHOLDS' RANCOR TO PURE LOVE.
Meanwhile, Benvolio and Mercutio receive a letter that will change everything. Tybalt has challenged Romeo.
TYBALT, THE KINSMAN TO OLD CAPULET, HATH SENT A LETTER TO HIS FATHER'S HOUSE.
A CHALLENGE, ON MY LIFE.
ROMEO WILL ANSWER IT.

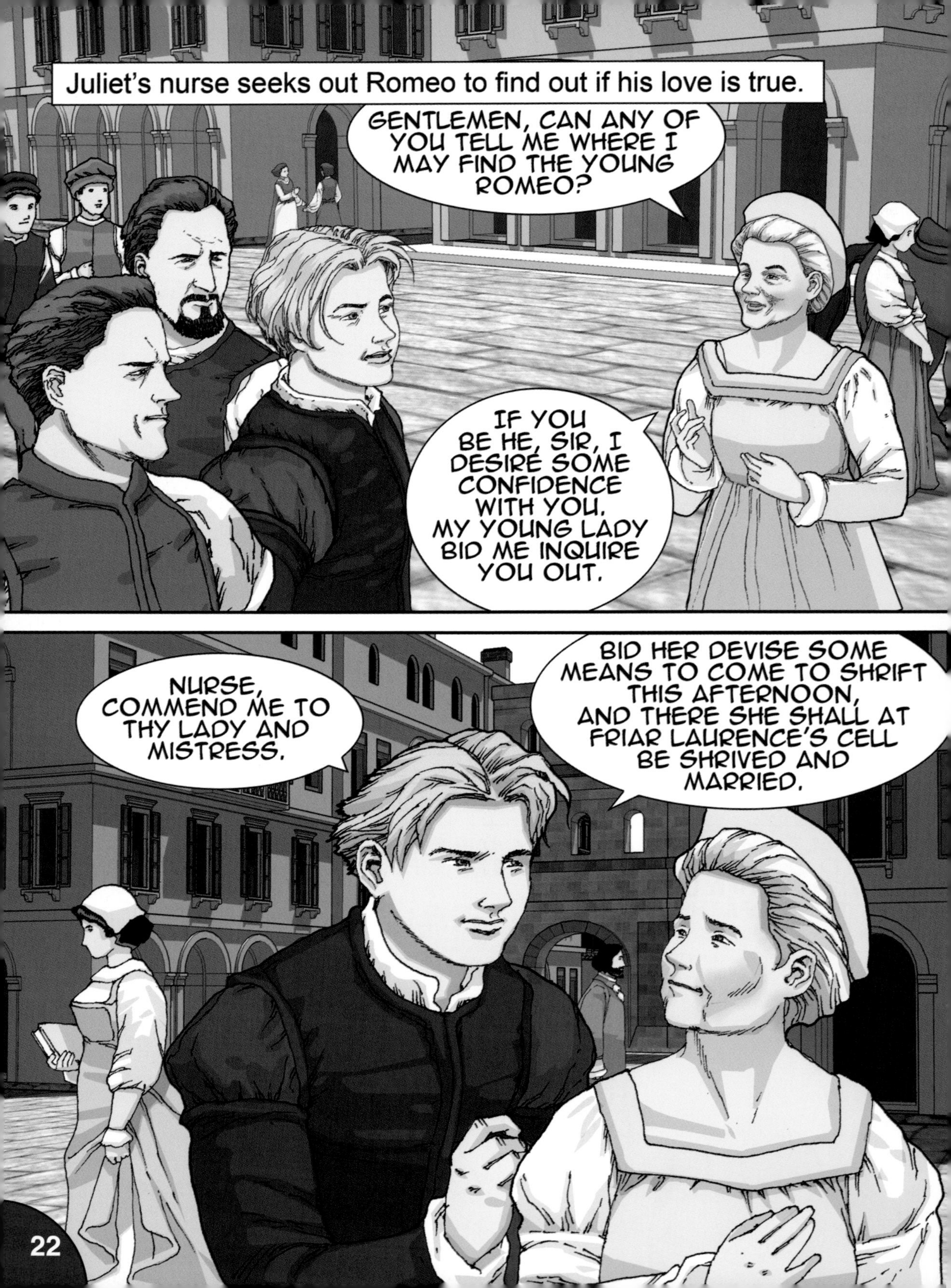
Juliet's nurse seeks out Romeo to find out if his love is true.
GENTLEMEN, CAN ANY OF YOU TELL ME WHERE I MAY FIND THE YOUNG ROMEO?
IF YOU BE HE, SIR, I DESIRE SOME CONFIDENCE WITH YOU. MY YOUNG LADY BID ME INQUIRE YOU OUT.
NURSE, COMMEND ME TO THY LADY AND MISTRESS.
BID HER DEVISE SOME MEANS TO COME TO SHRIFT THIS AFTERNOON, AND THERE SHE SHALL AT FRIAR LAURENCE'S CELL BE SHRIVED AND MARRIED.

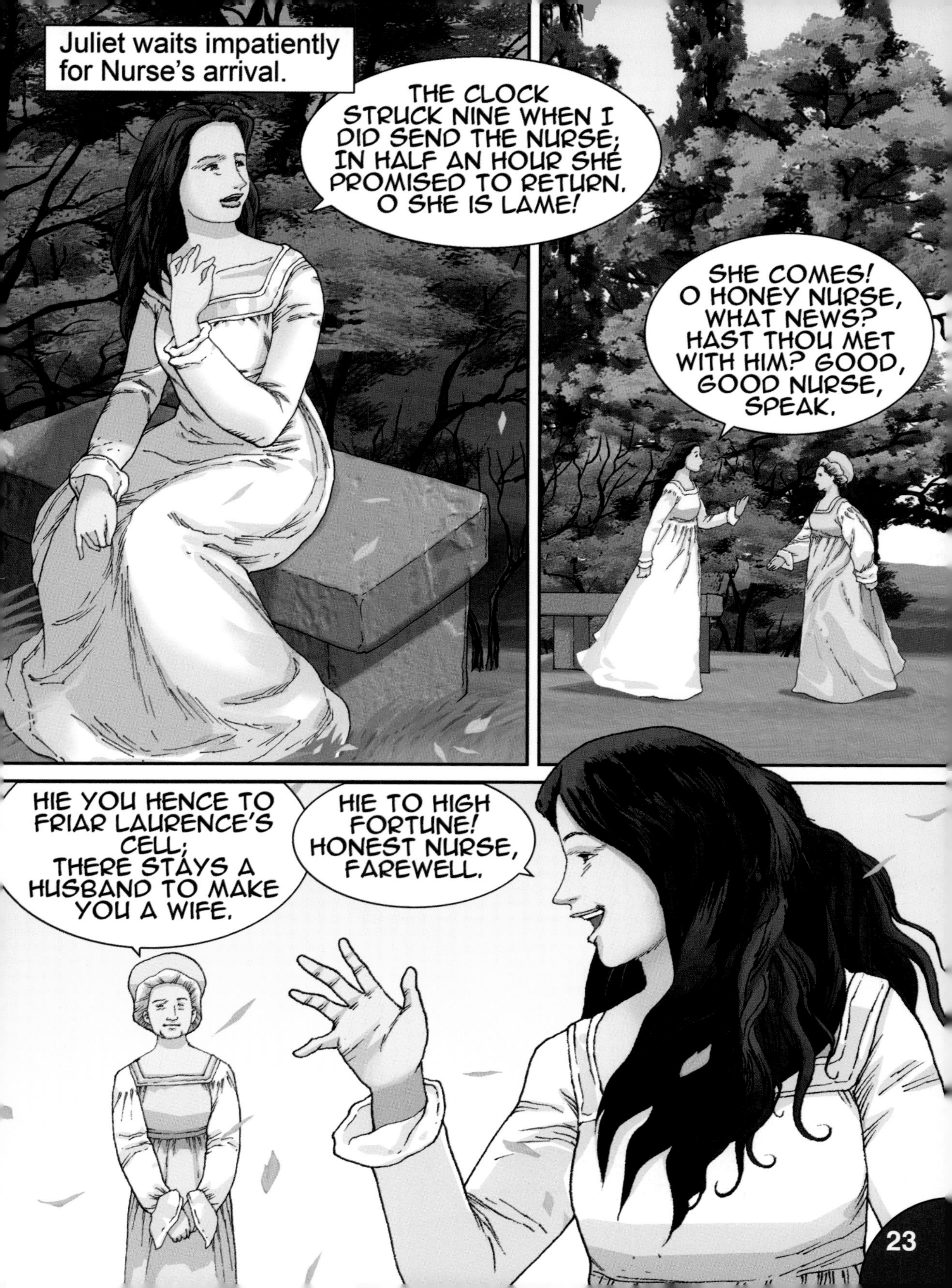
Juliet waits impatiently for Nurse's arrival.
THE CLOCK STRUCK NINE WHEN I DID SEND THE NURSE; IN HALF AN HOUR SHE PROMISED TO RETURN. O SHE IS LAME!
SHE COMES! O HONEY NURSE, WHAT NEWS? HAST THOU MET WITH HIM? GOOD, GOOD NURSE, SPEAK.
HIE YOU HENCE TO FRIAR LAURENCE'S CELL; THERE STAYS A HUSBAND TO MAKE YOU A WIFE.
HIE TO HIGH FORTUNE! HONEST NURSE, FAREWELL.

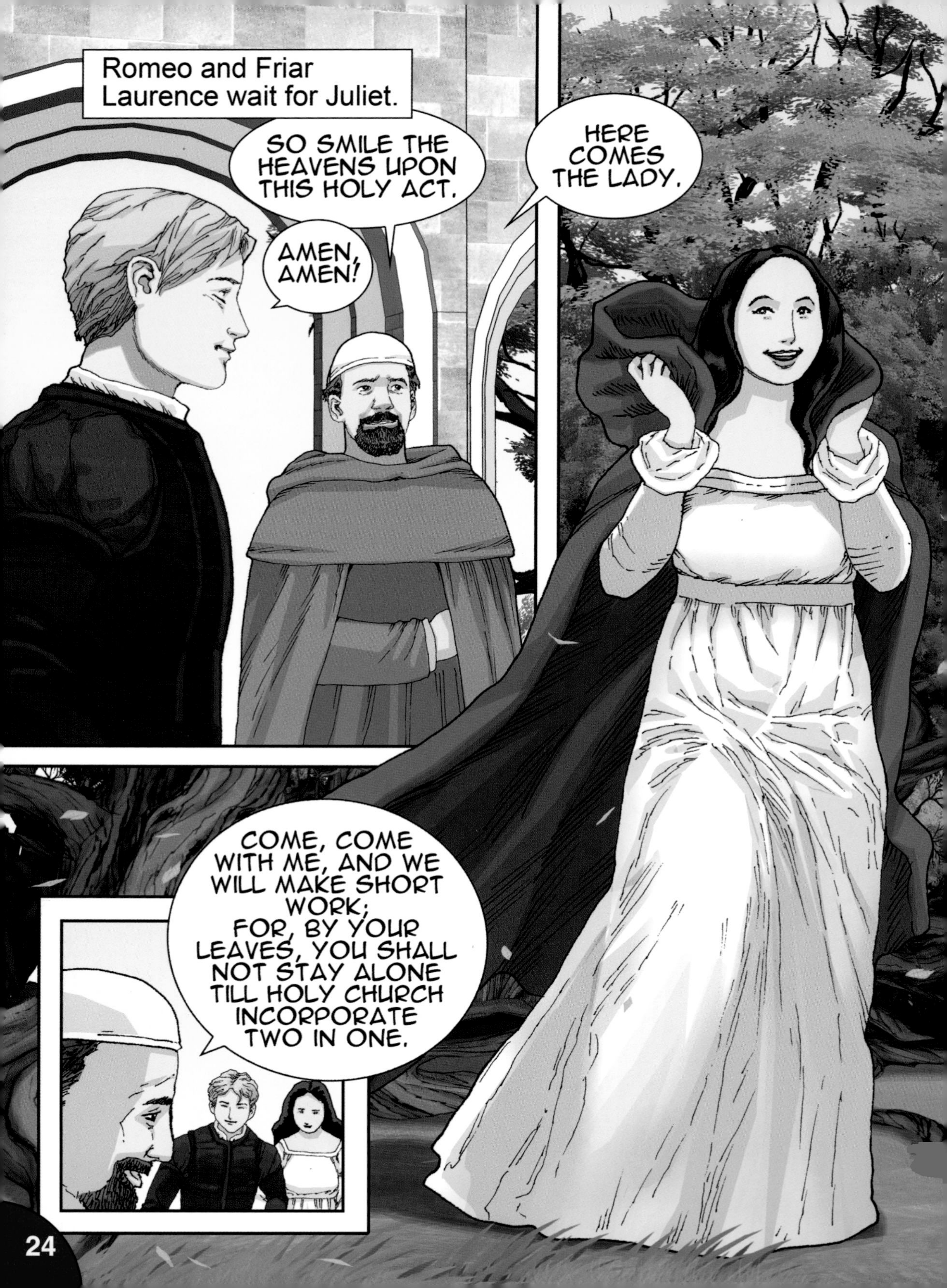
Romeo and Friar Laurence wait for Juliet.
SO SMILE THE HEAVENS UPON THIS HOLY ACT.
AMEN, AMEN!
HERE COMES THE LADY.
COME, COME WITH ME, AND WE WILL MAKE SHORT WORK; FOR, BY YOUR LEAVES, YOU SHALL NOT STAY ALONE TILL HOLY CHURCH INCORPORATE TWO IN ONE.

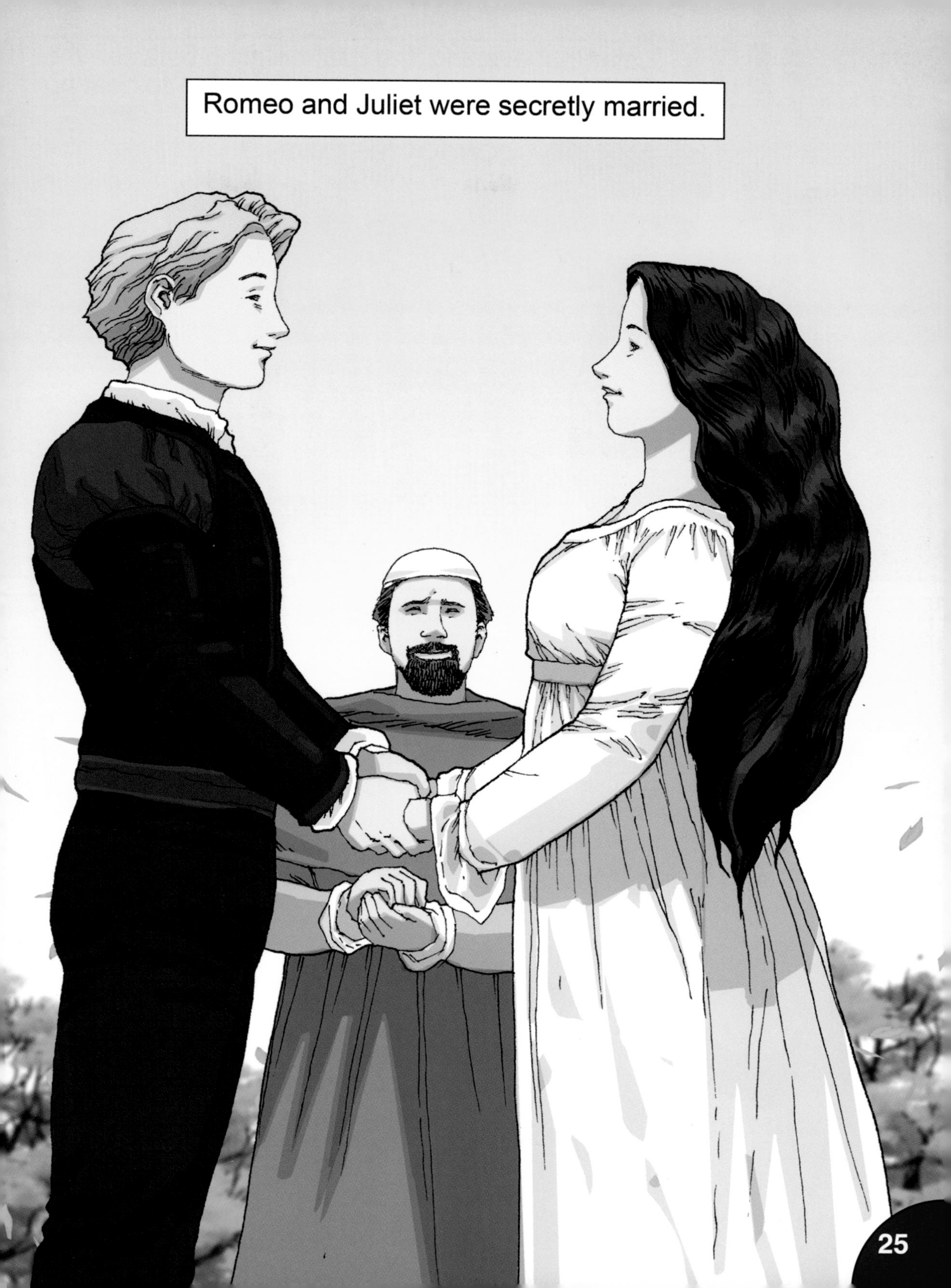
Romeo and Juliet were secretly married.

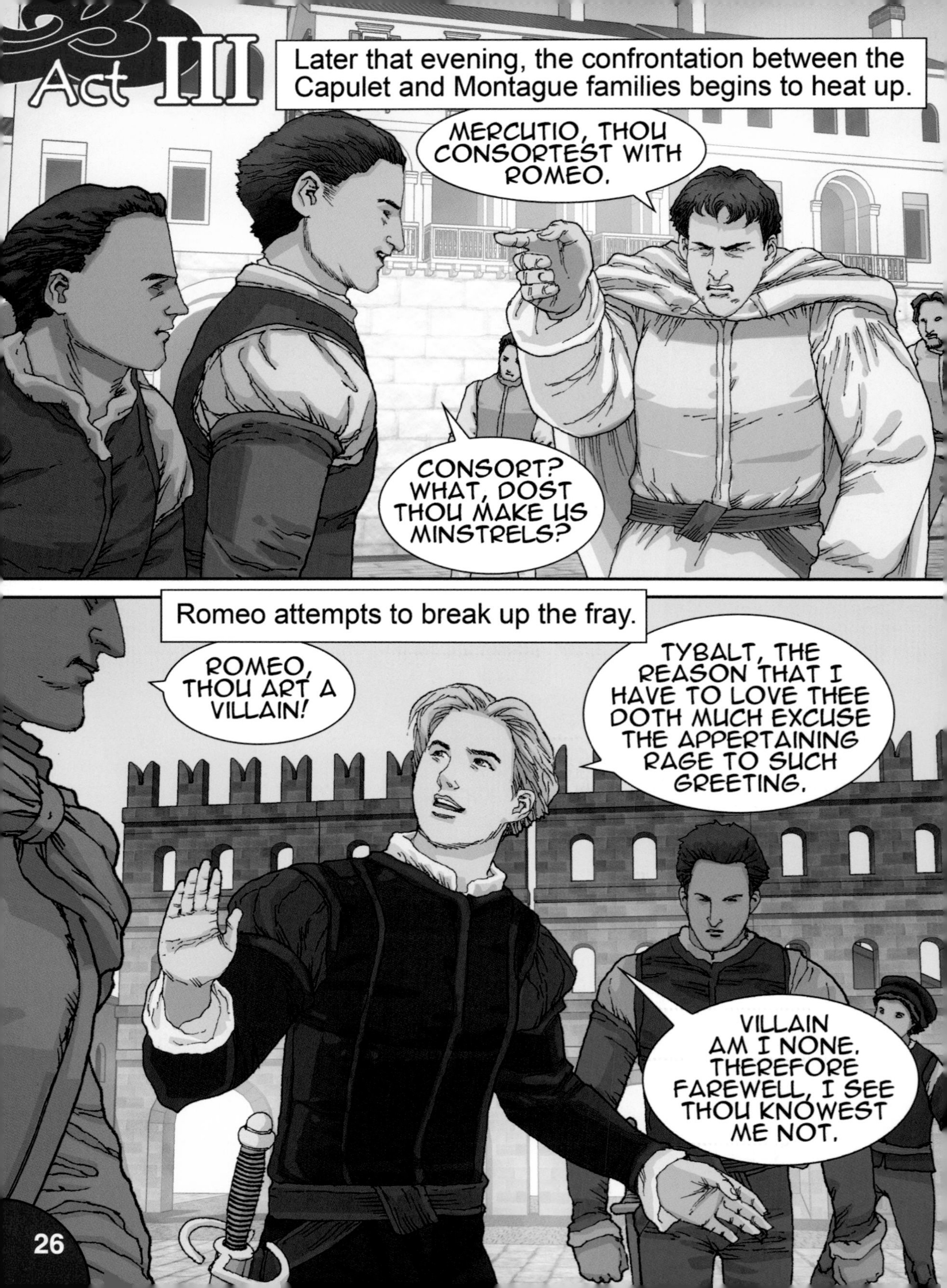
Act III
Later that evening, the confrontation between the Capulet and Montague families begins to heat up.
MERCUTIO, THOU CONSORTEST WITH ROMEO.
CONSORT? WHAT, DOST THOU MAKE US MINSTRELS?
Romeo attempts to break up the fray.
ROMEO, THOU ART A VILLAIN!
TYBALT, THE REASON THAT I HAVE TO LOVE THEE DOTH MUCH EXCUSE THE APPERTAINING RAGE TO SUCH GREETING.
VILLAIN AM I NONE. THEREFORE FAREWELL, I SEE THOU KNOWEST ME NOT.

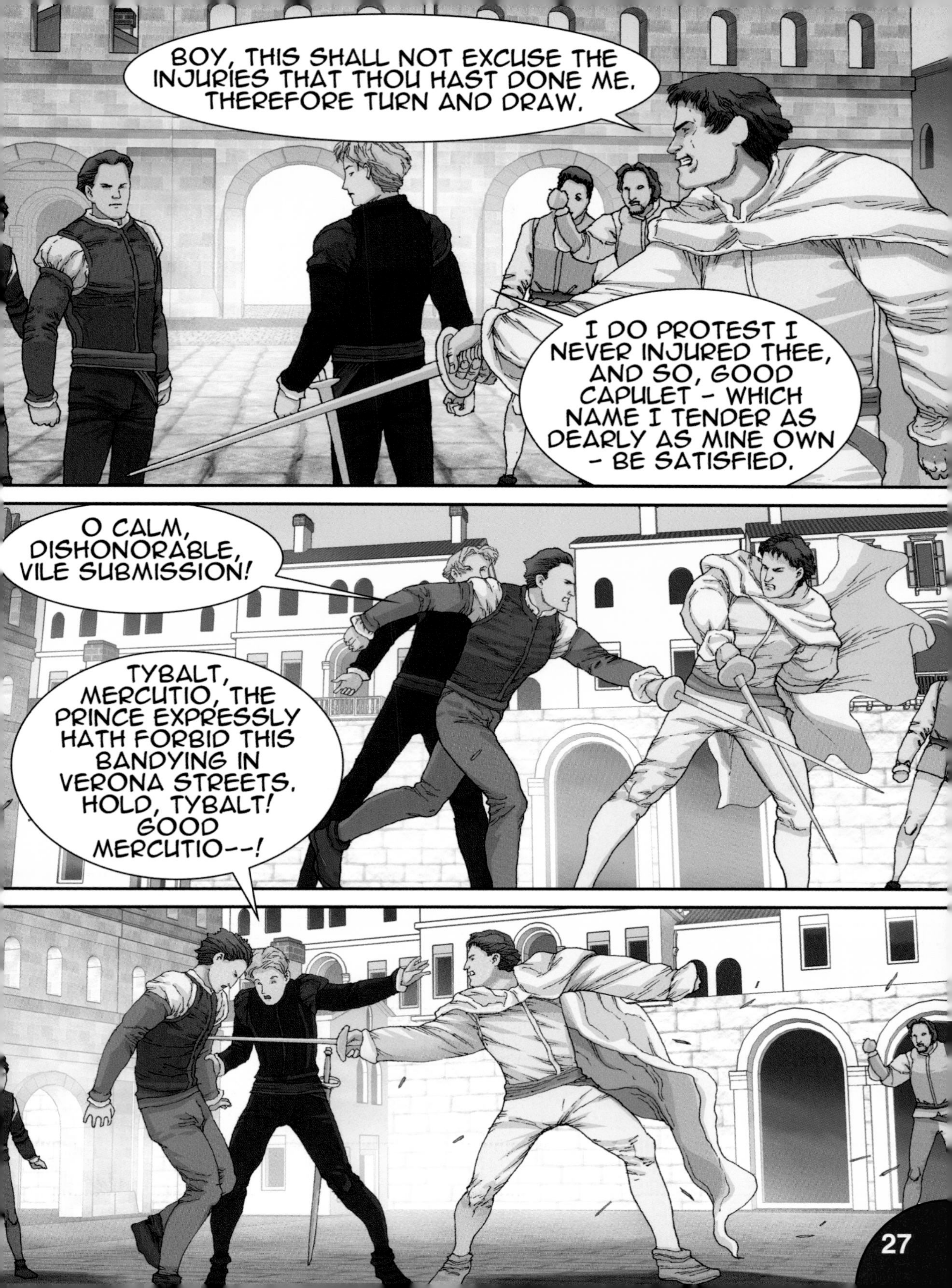
BOY, THIS SHALL NOT EXCUSE THE INJURIES THAT THOU HAST DONE ME. THEREFORE TURN AND DRAW.
I DO PROTEST I NEVER INJURED THEE, AND SO, GOOD CAPULET - WHICH NAME I TENDER AS DEARLY AS MINE OWN - BE SATISFIED.
O CALM, DISHONORABLE, VILE SUBMISSION!
TYBALT, MERCUTIO, THE PRINCE EXPRESSLY HATH FORBID THIS BANDYING IN VERONA STREETS. HOLD, TYBALT! GOOD MERCUTIO--!

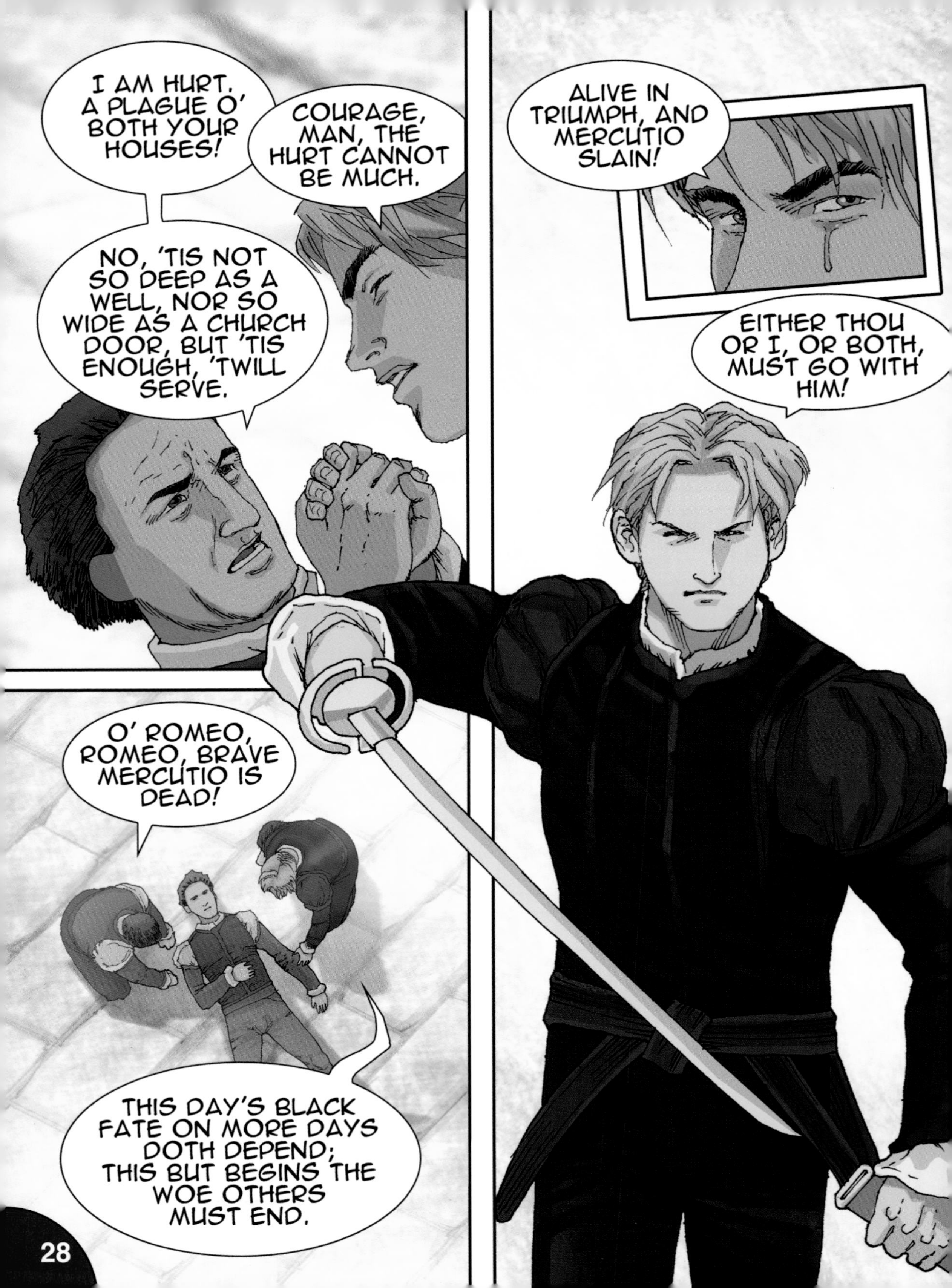
I AM HURT. A PLAGUE O' BOTH YOUR HOUSES!
COURAGE, MAN, THE HURT CANNOT BE MUCH.
NO, 'TIS NOT SO DEEP AS A WELL, NOR SO WIDE AS A CHURCH DOOR, BUT 'TIS ENOUGH, 'TWILL SERVE.
O' ROMEO, ROMEO, BRAVE MERCUTIO IS DEAD!
THIS DAY'S BLACK FATE ON MORE DAYS DOTH DEPEND; THIS BUT BEGINS THE WOE OTHERS MUST END.
ALIVE IN TRIUMPH, AND MERCUTIO SLAIN!
EITHER THOU OR I, OR BOTH, MUST GO WITH HIM!

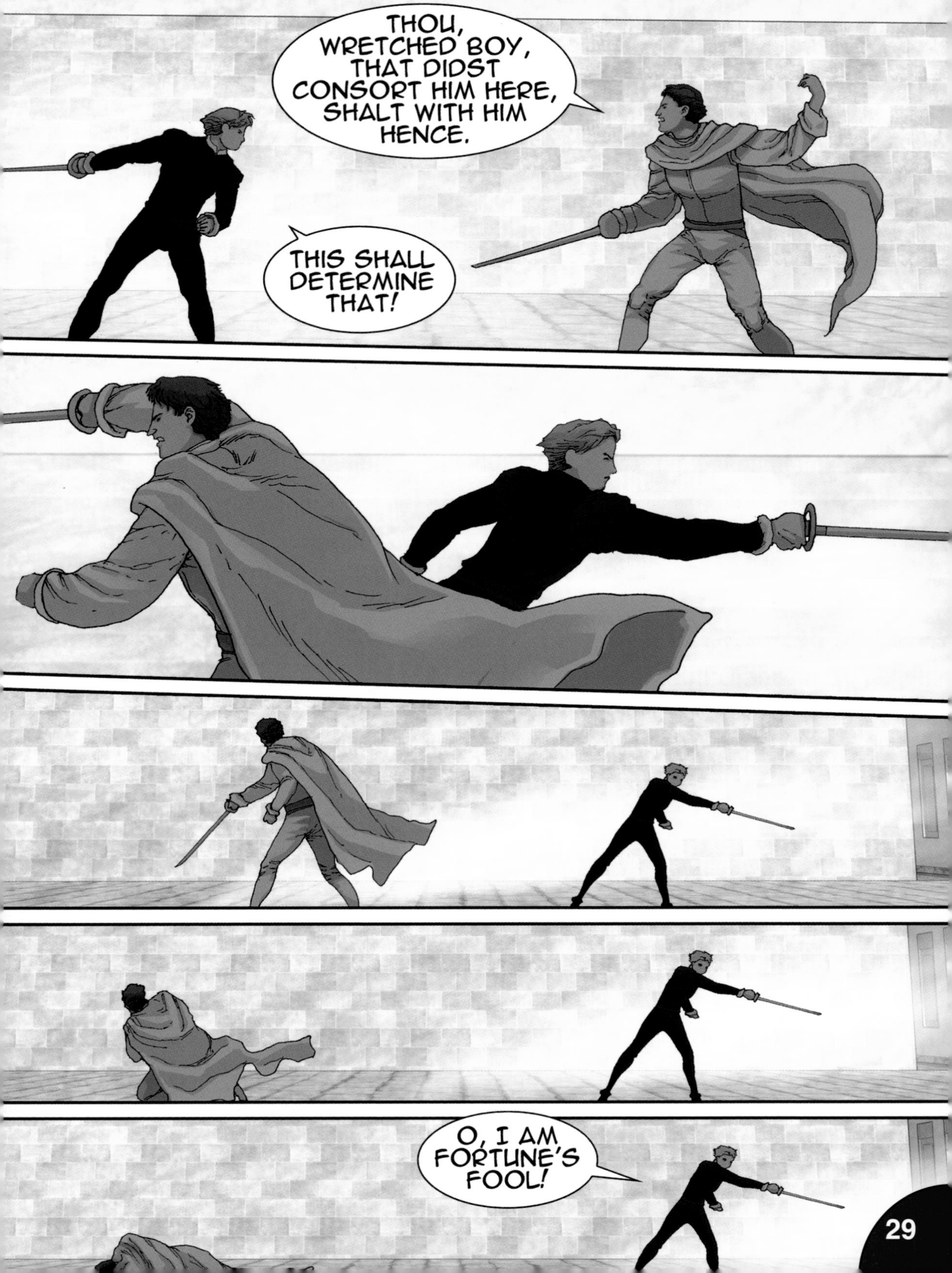
THOU, WRETCHED BOY, THAT DIDST CONSORT HIM HERE, SHALT WITH HIM HENCE.
THIS SHALL DETERMINE THAT!
O, I AM FORTUNE'S FOOL!

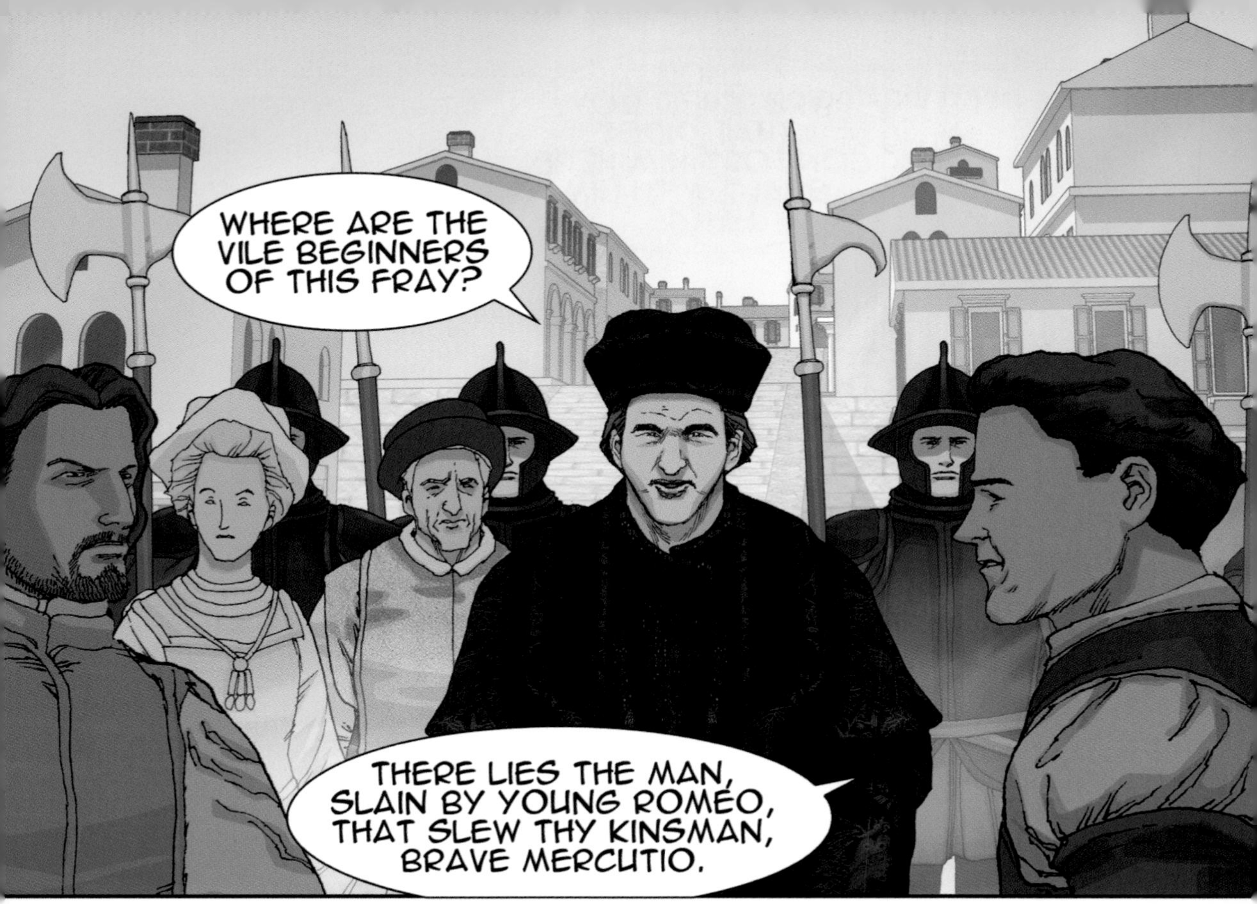
WHERE ARE THE VILE BEGINNERS OF THIS FRAY?
THERE LIES THE MAN, SLAIN BY YOUNG ROMEO, THAT SLEW THY KINSMAN, BRAVE MERCUTIO.

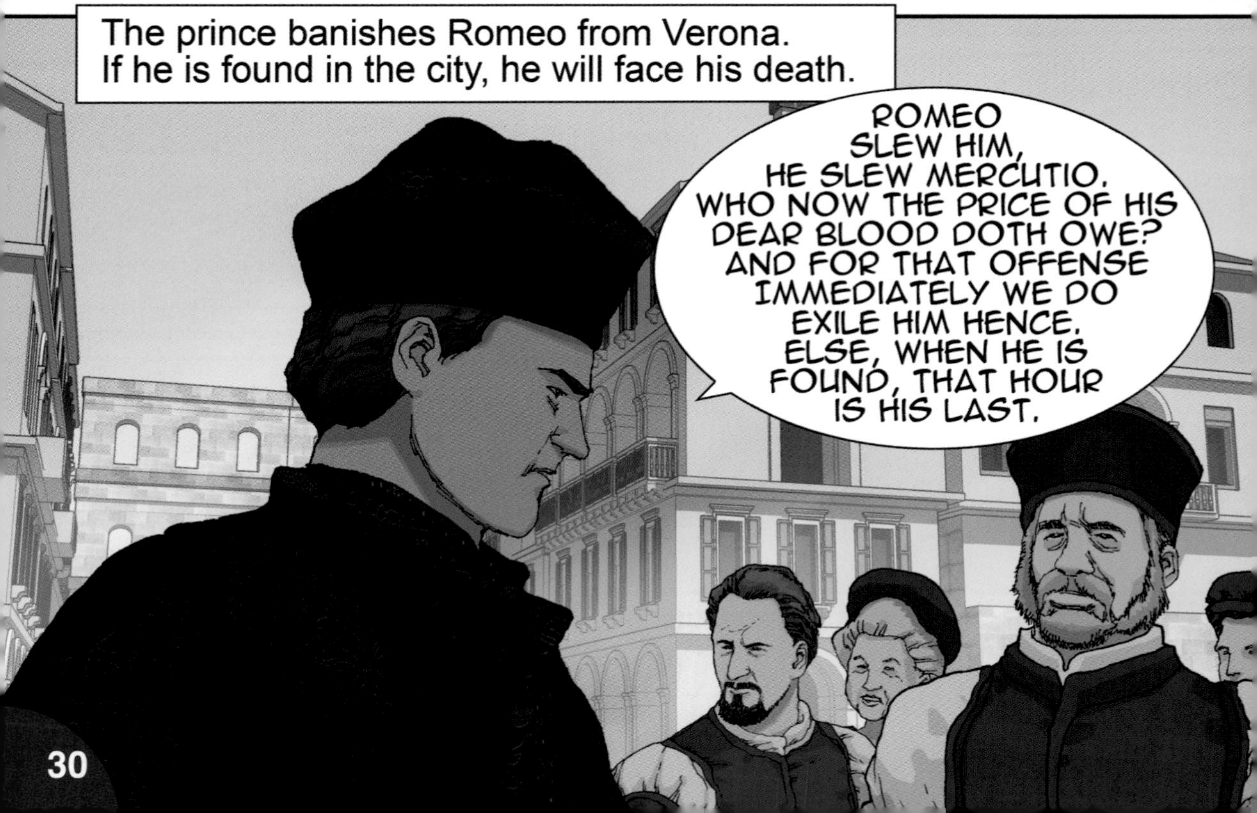
The prince banishes Romeo from Verona. If he is found in the city, he will face his death.
ROMEO SLEW HIM, HE SLEW MERCUTIO. WHO NOW THE PRICE OF HIS DEAR BLOOD DOTH OWE? AND FOR THAT OFFENSE IMMEDIATELY WE DO EXILE HIM HENCE. ELSE, WHEN HE IS FOUND, THAT HOUR IS HIS LAST.

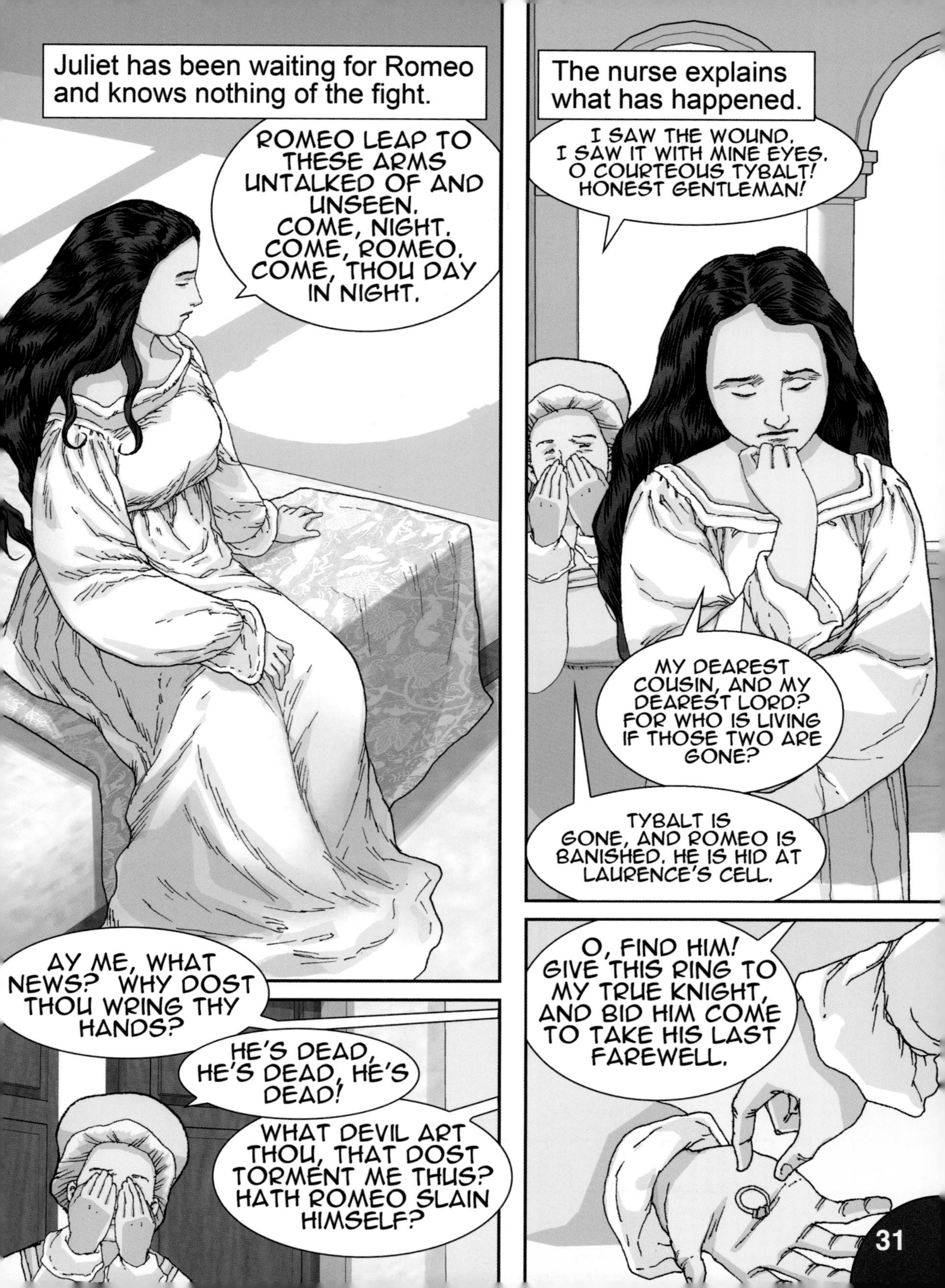

Juliet has been waiting for Romeo and knows nothing of the fight.
ROMEO LEAP TO THESE ARMS UNTALKED OF AND UNSEEN. COME, NIGHT. COME, ROMEO. COME, THOU DAY IN NIGHT.
AY ME, WHAT NEWS? WHY DOST THOU WRING THY HANDS?
HE'S DEAD, HE'S DEAD, HE'S DEAD!
WHAT DEVIL ART THOU, THAT DOST TORMENT ME THUS? HATH ROMEO SLAIN HIMSELF?
The nurse explains what has happened.
I SAW THE WOUND. I SAW IT WITH MINE EYES. O COURTEOUS TYBALT! HONEST GENTLEMAN!
MY DEAREST COUSIN, AND MY DEAREST LORD? FOR WHO IS LIVING IF THOSE TWO ARE GONE?
TYBALT IS GONE, AND ROMEO IS BANISHED. HE IS HID AT LAURENCE'S CELL.
O, FIND HIM! GIVE THIS RING TO MY TRUE KNIGHT, AND BID HIM COME TO TAKE HIS LAST FAREWELL.

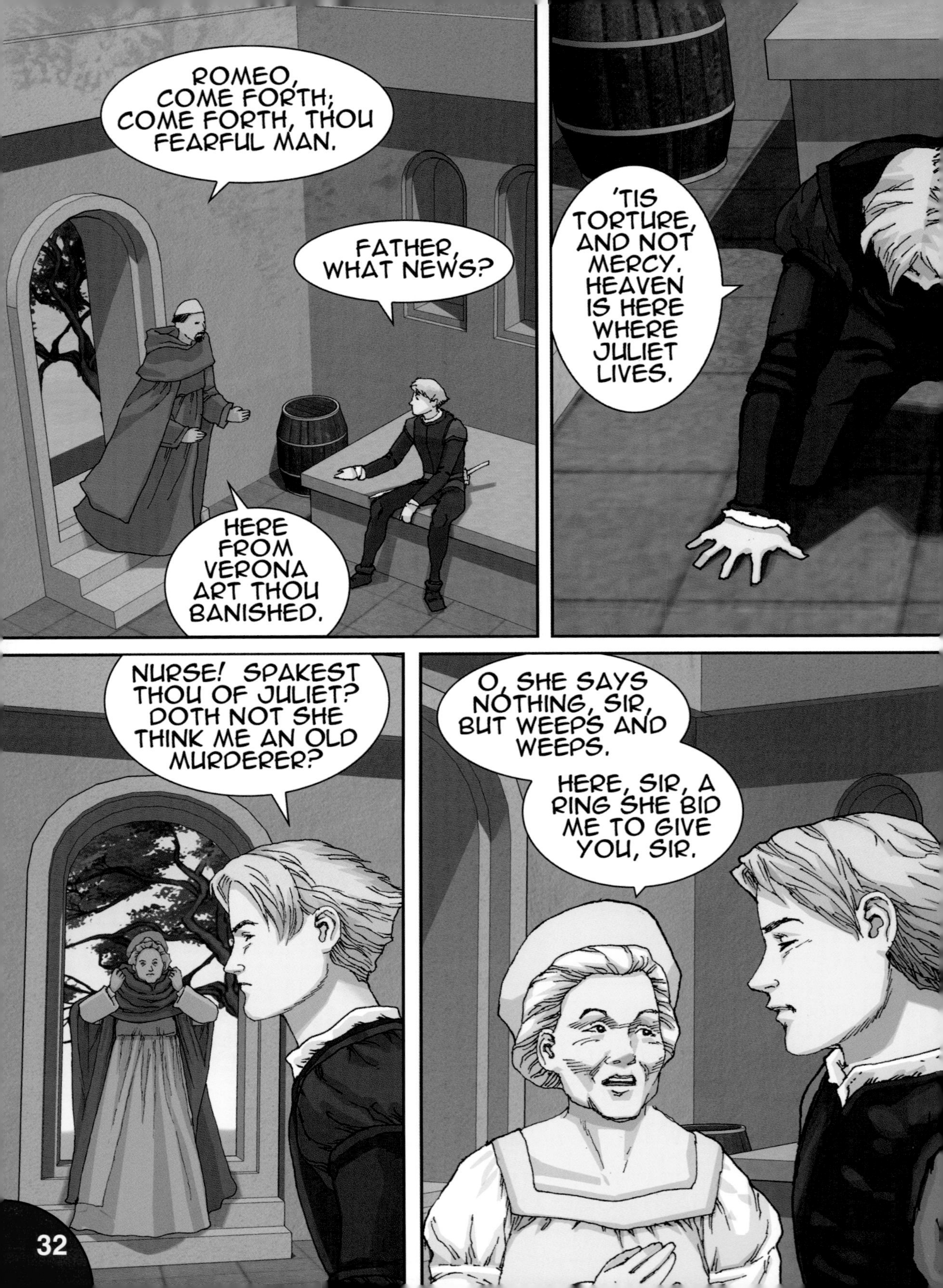
ROMEO, COME FORTH; COME FORTH, THOU FEARFUL MAN.
FATHER, WHAT NEWS?
HERE FROM VERONA ART THOU BANISHED.
'TIS TORTURE, AND NOT MERCY. HEAVEN IS HERE WHERE JULIET LIVES.
NURSE! SPAKEST THOU OF JULIET? DOTH NOT SHE THINK ME AN OLD MURDERER?
O, SHE SAYS NOTHING, SIR, BUT WEEPS AND WEEPS.
HERE, SIR, A RING SHE BID ME TO GIVE YOU, SIR.

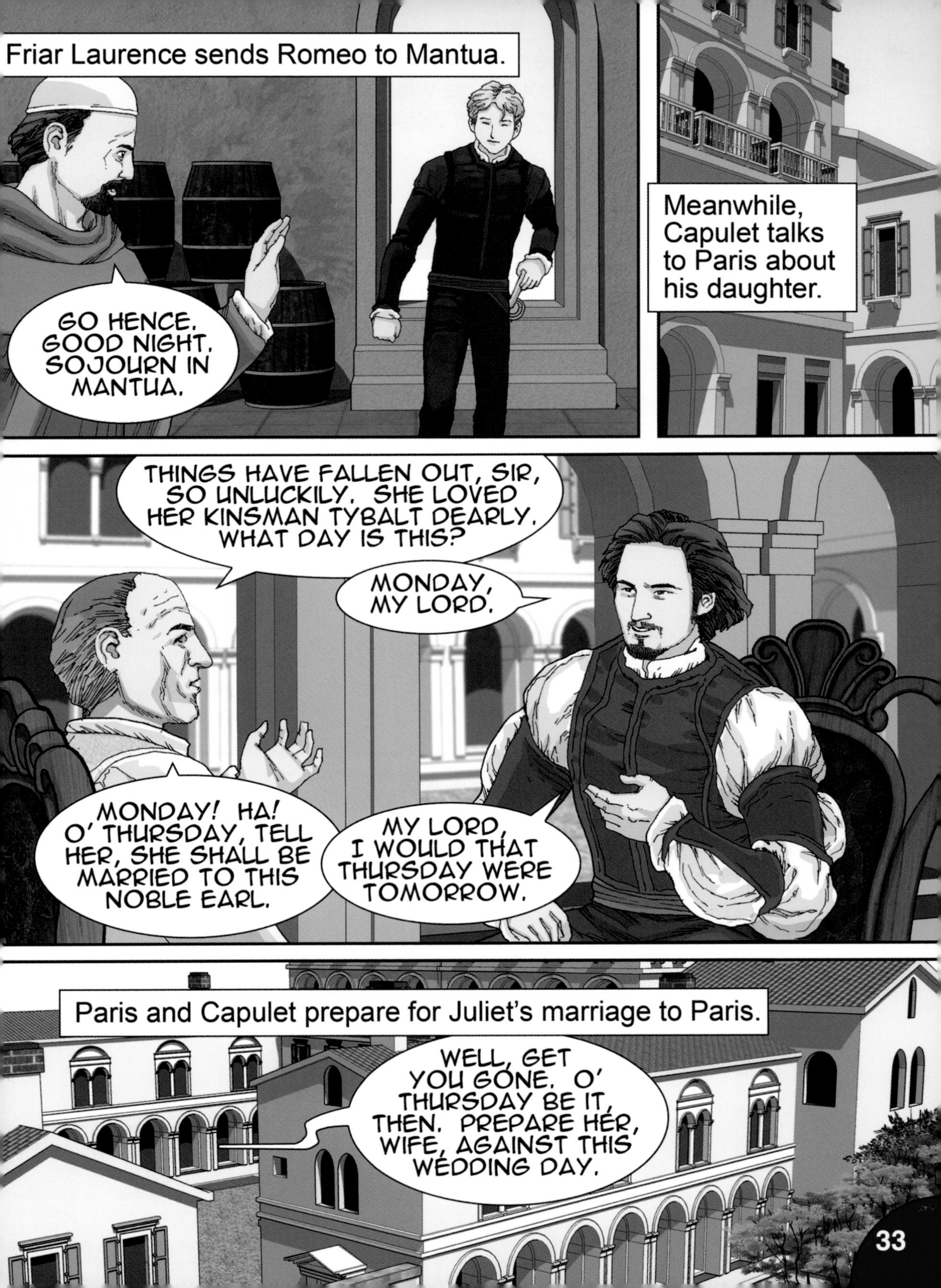
Friar Laurence sends Romeo to Mantua.
GO HENCE. GOOD NIGHT. SOJOURN IN MANTUA.
Meanwhile, Capulet talks to Paris about his daughter.
THINGS HAVE FALLEN OUT, SIR, SO UNLUCKILY. SHE LOVED HER KINSMAN TYBALT DEARLY. WHAT DAY IS THIS?
MONDAY, MY LORD.
MONDAY! HA! O' THURSDAY, TELL HER, SHE SHALL BE MARRIED TO THIS NOBLE EARL.
MY LORD, I WOULD THAT THURSDAY WERE TOMORROW.
Paris and Capulet prepare for Juliet's marriage to Paris.
WELL, GET YOU GONE. O' THURSDAY BE IT, THEN. PREPARE HER, WIFE, AGAINST THIS WEDDING DAY.

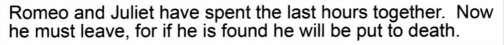

Romeo and Juliet have spent the last hours together. Now he must leave, for if he is found he will be put to death.

IT IS THE LARK THAT SINGS SO OUT OF TUNE, STRAINING HARSH DISCORDS AND UNPLEASING SHARPS. FOR SHE DIVIDETH US.

MORE LIGHT AND LIGHT, MORE DARK AND DARK OUR WOES!

JULIET! YOUR LADY MOTHER IS COMING TO YOUR CHAMBER.

THEN WINDOW, LET DAY IN, AND LET LIFE OUT.

FAREWELL, FAREWELL! ONE KISS, AND I'LL DESCEND.

O, THINK'ST THOU WE SHALL EVER MEET AGAIN?

I DOUBT IT NOT, AND ALL THESE WOES SHALL SERVE FOR SWEET DISCOURSES IN OUR TIMES TO COME.

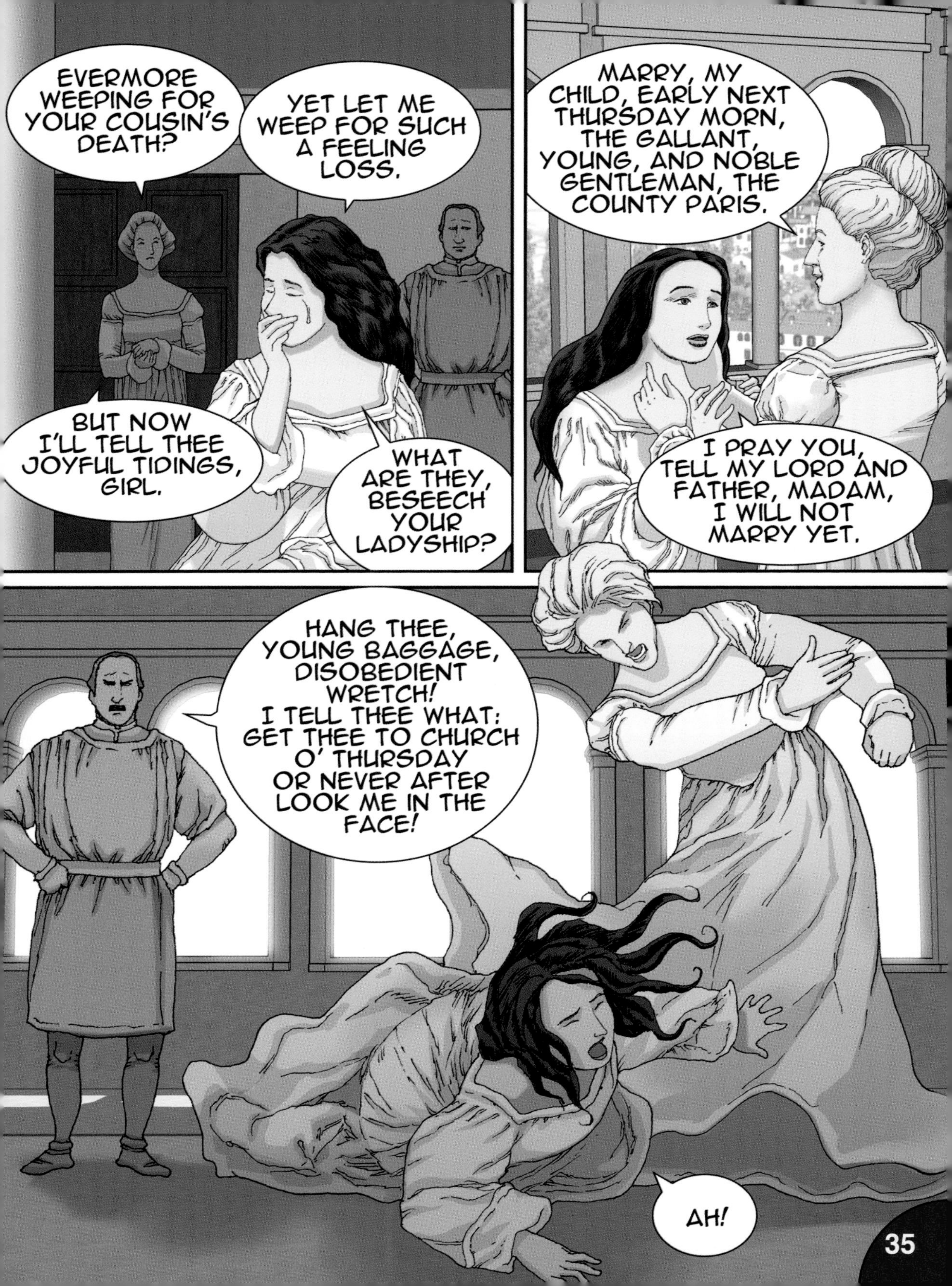
EVERMORE WEEPING FOR YOUR COUSIN'S DEATH?
YET LET ME WEEP FOR SUCH A FEELING LOSS.
BUT NOW I'LL TELL THEE JOYFUL TIDINGS, GIRL.
WHAT ARE THEY, BESEECH YOUR LADYSHIP?
MARRY, MY CHILD, EARLY NEXT THURSDAY MORN, THE GALLANT, YOUNG, AND NOBLE GENTLEMAN, THE COUNTY PARIS.
I PRAY YOU, TELL MY LORD AND FATHER, MADAM, I WILL NOT MARRY YET.
HANG THEE, YOUNG BAGGAGE, DISOBEDIENT WRETCH! I TELL THEE WHAT: GET THEE TO CHURCH O' THURSDAY OR NEVER AFTER LOOK ME IN THE FACE!
AH!

Act IV

Juliet escapes to Friar Laurence for counsel about the situation.

COME WEEP WITH ME, PAST HOPE, PAST CURE, PAST HELP!

AH JULIET, I ALREADY KNOW THY GRIEF; IT STRAINS ME PAST THE COMPASS OF MY WITS.

BID ME GO INTO A NEW-MADE GRAVE AND HIDE ME WITH A DEAD MAN IN HIS TOMB--

Together they develop a plan.

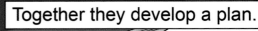

HOLD THEN. GO HOME, BE MERRY, GIVE CONSENT TO MARRY PARIS, WEDNESDAY IS TOMORROW.

TOMORROW NIGHT LOOK THAT THOU LIE ALONE. TAKE THOU THIS VIAL, BEING THEN IN BED, WHEN PRESENTLY THROUGH ALL THY VEINS SHALL RUN A COLD AND DROWSY HUMOR; FOR NO PULSE, NO WARMTH, NO BREATH SHALL TESTIFY THOU LIVEST.

THOU SHALT CONTINUE TWO-AND-FORTY HOURS, AND THEN AWAKE AS FROM A PLEASANT SLEEP. THOU SHALT BE BORNE TO THAT SAME ANCIENT VAULT WHERE ALL THE KINDRED OF THE CAPULETS LIE.

SHALL ROMEO BY MY LETTERS KNOW OUR DRIFT, AND HITHER SHALL HE COME; AND HE AND I WILL WATCH THY WAKING, AND THAT VERY NIGHT SHALL ROMEO BEAR THEE TO MANTUA.

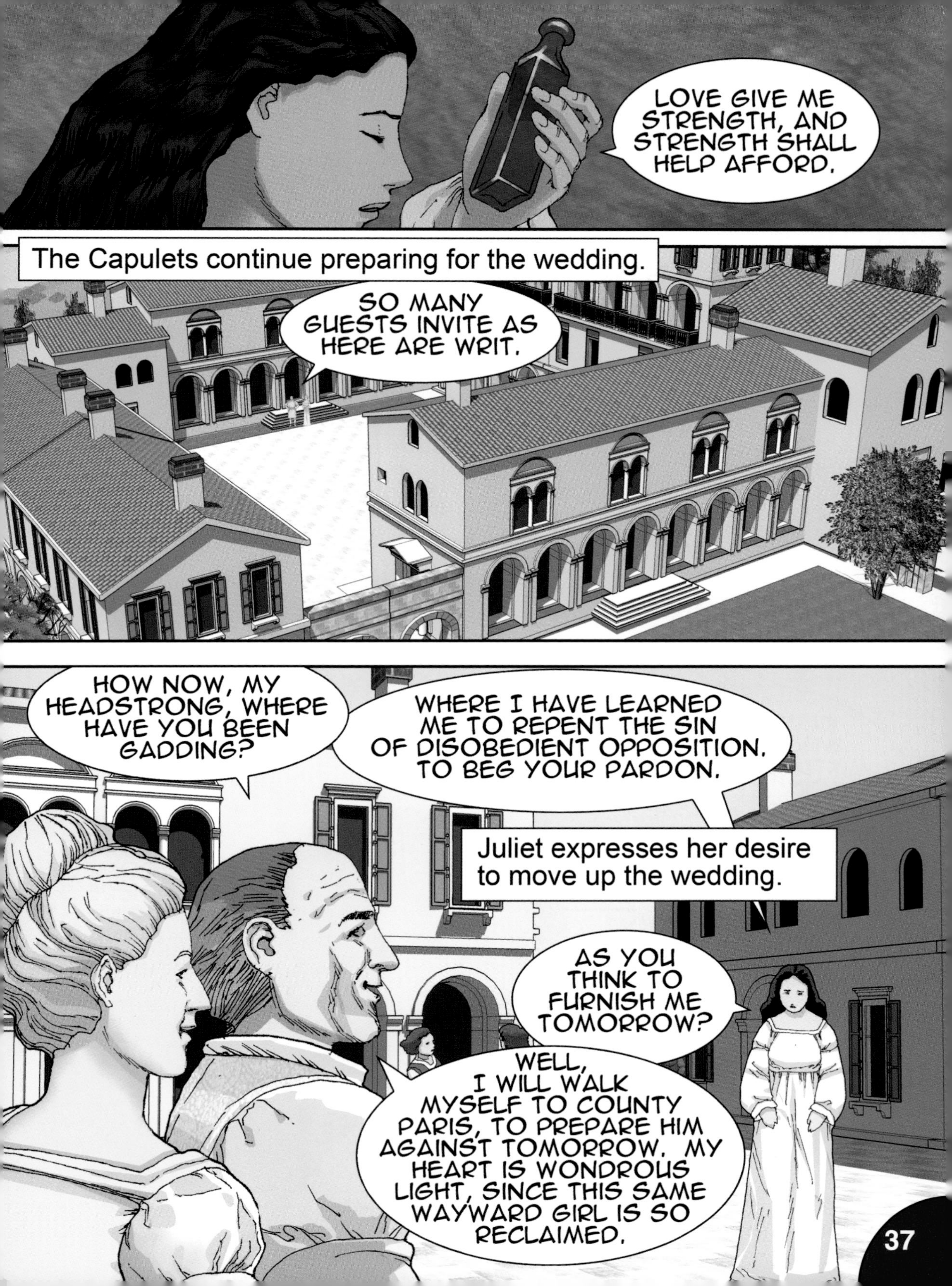
LOVE GIVE ME STRENGTH, AND STRENGTH SHALL HELP AFFORD.
The Capulets continue preparing for the wedding.
SO MANY GUESTS INVITE AS HERE ARE WRIT.
HOW NOW, MY HEADSTRONG, WHERE HAVE YOU BEEN GADDING?
WHERE I HAVE LEARNED ME TO REPENT THE SIN OF DISOBEDIENT OPPOSITION. TO BEG YOUR PARDON.
Juliet expresses her desire to move up the wedding.
AS YOU THINK TO FURNISH ME TOMORROW?
WELL, I WILL WALK MYSELF TO COUNTY PARIS, TO PREPARE HIM AGAINST TOMORROW. MY HEART IS WONDROUS LIGHT, SINCE THIS SAME WAYWARD GIRL IS SO RECLAIMED.

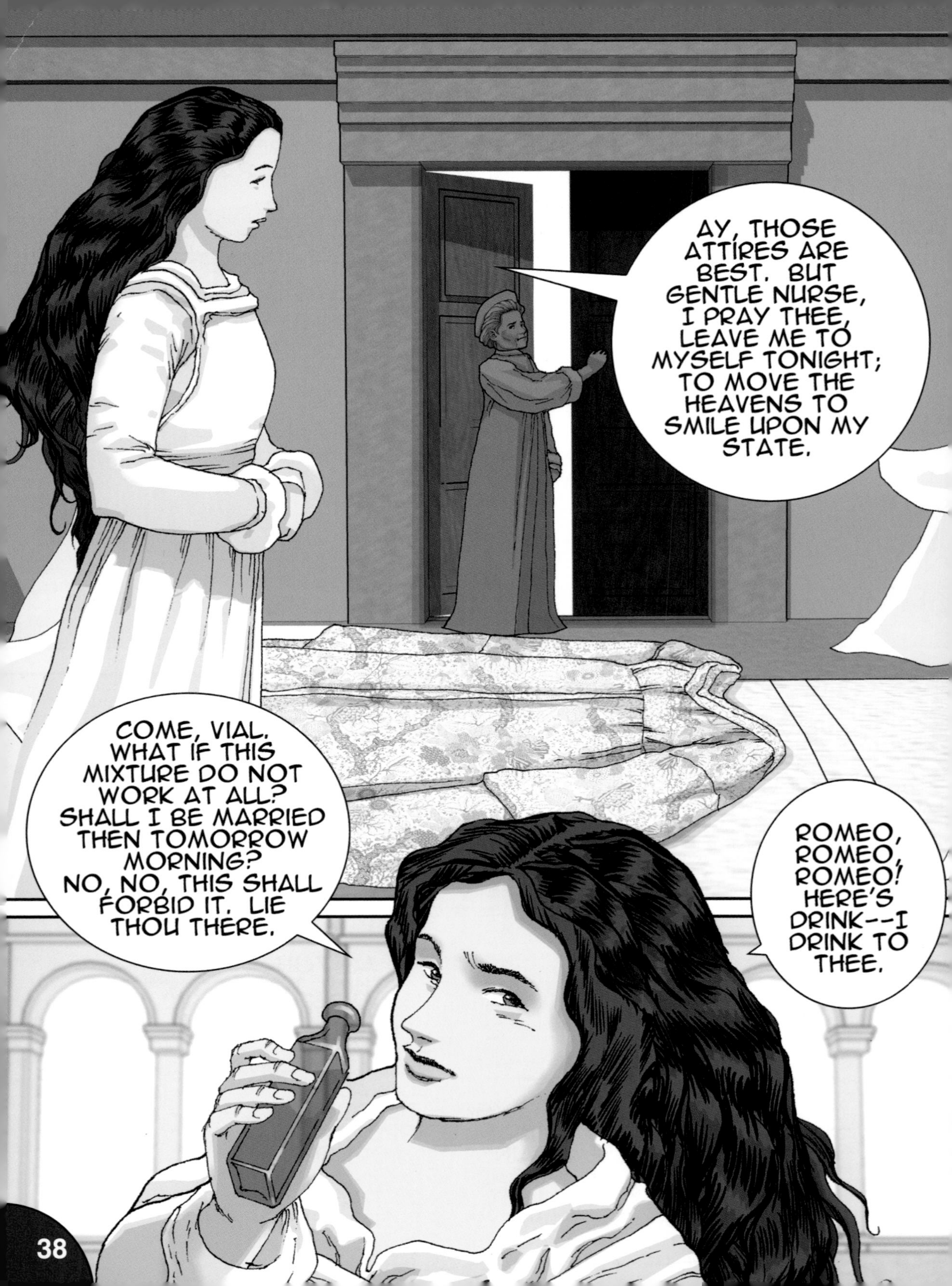
AY, THOSE ATTIRES ARE BEST. BUT GENTLE NURSE, I PRAY THEE, LEAVE ME TO MYSELF TONIGHT; TO MOVE THE HEAVENS TO SMILE UPON MY STATE.
COME, VIAL. WHAT IF THIS MIXTURE DO NOT WORK AT ALL? SHALL I BE MARRIED THEN TOMORROW MORNING? NO, NO, THIS SHALL FORBID IT. LIE THOU THERE.
ROMEO, ROMEO, ROMEO! HERE'S DRINK--I DRINK TO THEE.

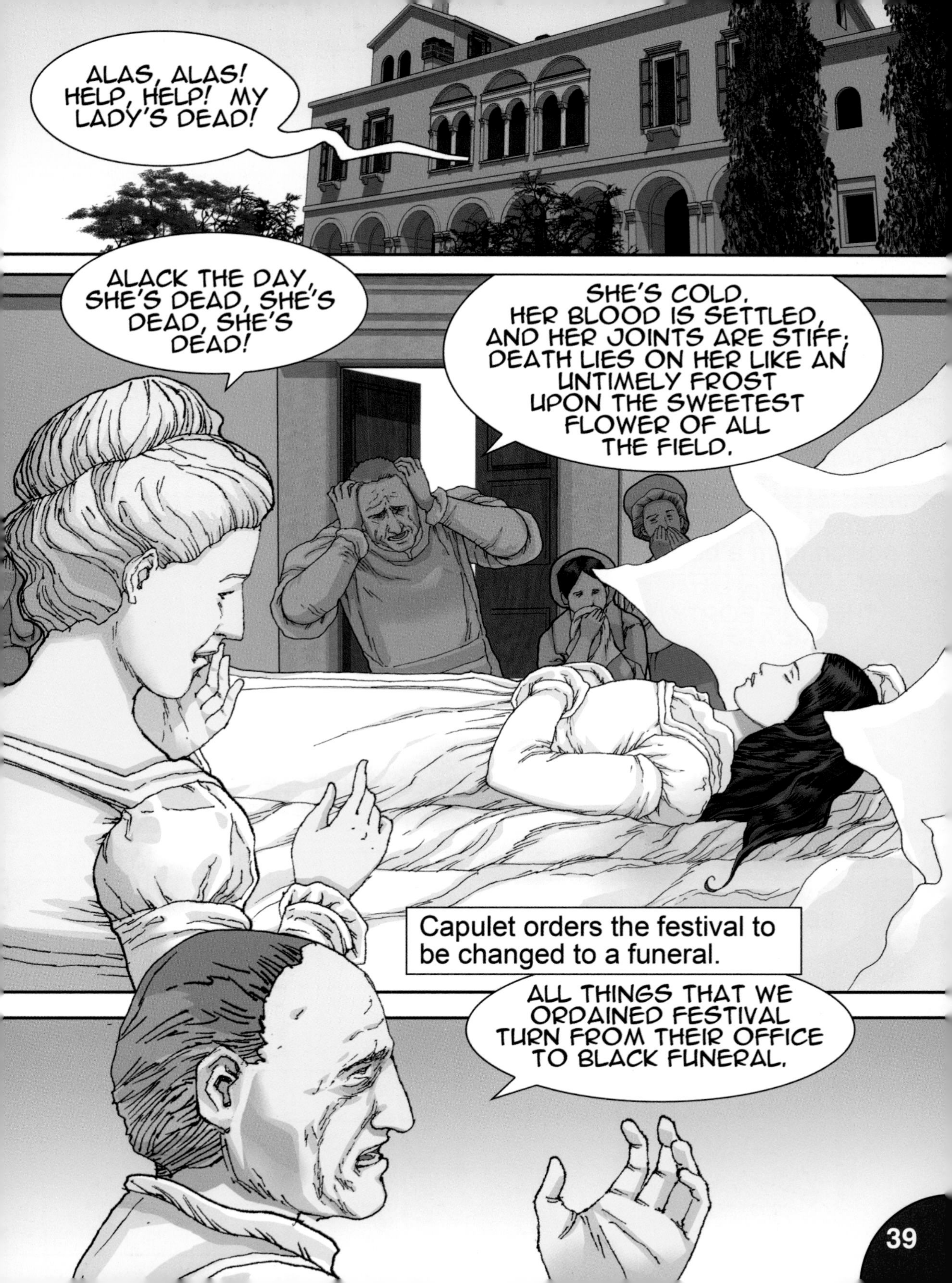
ALAS, ALAS! HELP, HELP! MY LADY'S DEAD!
ALACK THE DAY, SHE'S DEAD, SHE'S DEAD, SHE'S DEAD!
SHE'S COLD. HER BLOOD IS SETTLED, AND HER JOINTS ARE STIFF; DEATH LIES ON HER LIKE AN UNTIMELY FROST UPON THE SWEETEST FLOWER OF ALL THE FIELD.
Capulet orders the festival to be changed to a funeral.
ALL THINGS THAT WE ORDAINED FESTIVAL TURN FROM THEIR OFFICE TO BLACK FUNERAL.

Romeo's servant, Balthasar, brings news of Juliet's death to Romeo in Mantua.

NEWS FROM VERONA! HOW NOW, BALTHASAR? HOW DOTH MY LADY?

HER BODY SLEEPS IN CAPEL'S MONUMENT, AND HER IMMORTAL PART WITH ANGELS LIVES. O, PARDON ME FOR BRINGING THESE ILL NEWS.

LEAVE ME, AND DO THE THING I BID THEE DO.

Romeo buys some poison from a beggar.

HOLD, THERE IS FORTY DUCATS.

LET ME HAVE A DRAM OF POISON, SUCH SOON-SPEEDING GEAR AS WILL DISPERSE ITSELF THROUGH ALL THE VEINS THAT THE LIFE-WEARY TAKER MAY FALL DEAD.

TO JULIET'S GRAVE, FOR THERE I MUST USE THEE.

In Verona, Friar Laurence receives news of the letter he sent to Romeo.

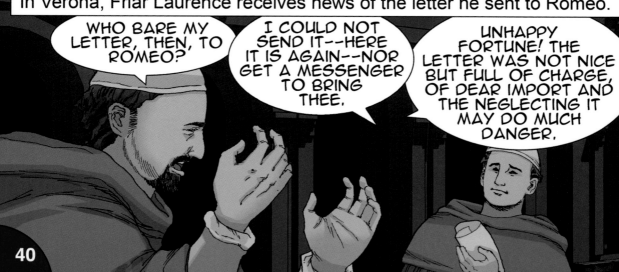

WHO BARE MY LETTER, THEN, TO ROMEO?

I COULD NOT SEND IT--HERE IT IS AGAIN--NOR GET A MESSENGER TO BRING THEE.

UNHAPPY FORTUNE! THE LETTER WAS NOT NICE BUT FULL OF CHARGE, OF DEAR IMPORT AND THE NEGLECTING IT MAY DO MUCH DANGER.

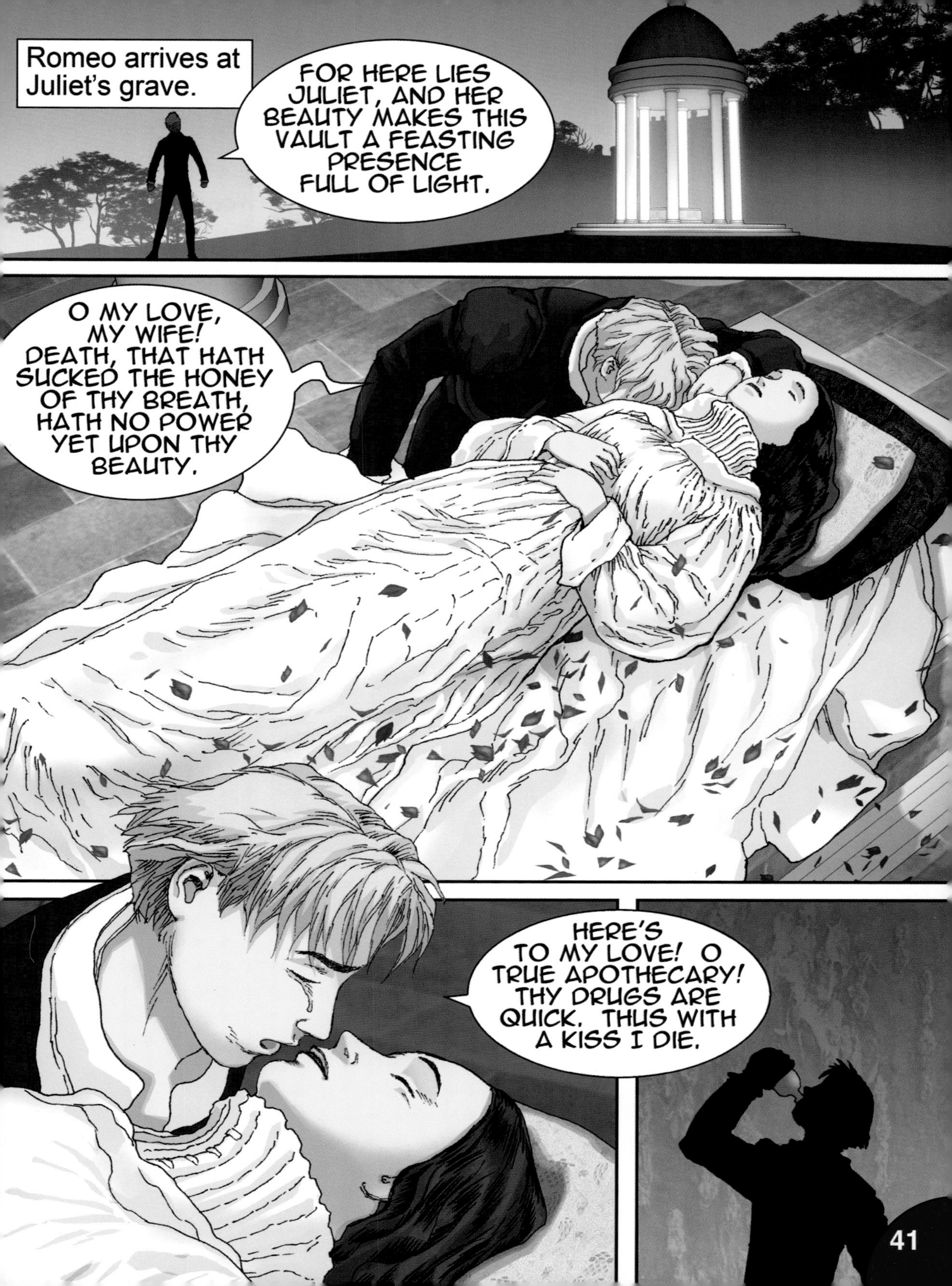
Romeo arrives at Juliet's grave.
FOR HERE LIES JULIET, AND HER BEAUTY MAKES THIS VAULT A FEASTING PRESENCE FULL OF LIGHT.
O MY LOVE, MY WIFE! DEATH, THAT HATH SUCKED THE HONEY OF THY BREATH, HATH NO POWER YET UPON THY BEAUTY.
HERE'S TO MY LOVE! O TRUE APOTHECARY! THY DRUGS ARE QUICK. THUS WITH A KISS I DIE.

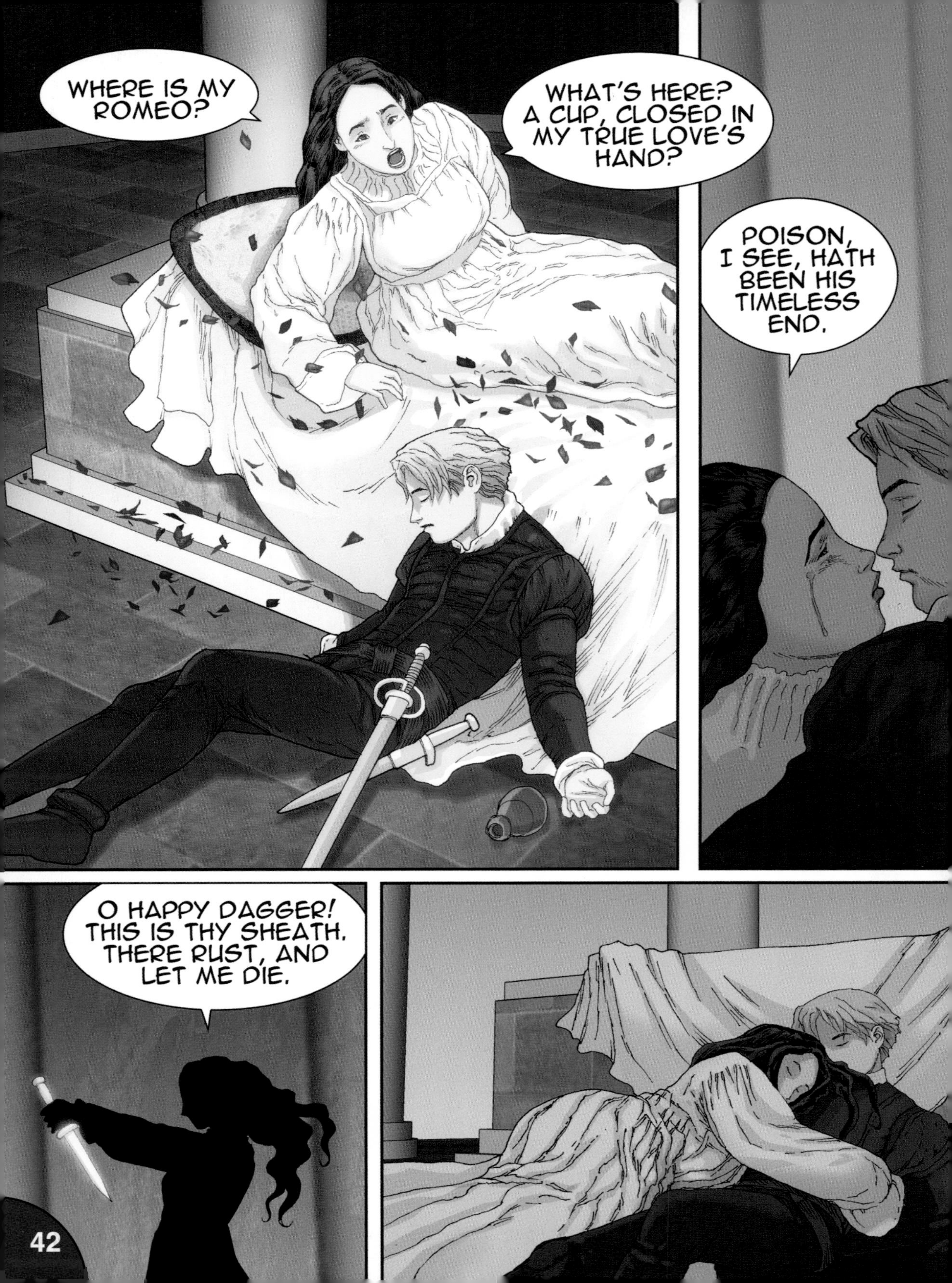
WHERE IS MY ROMEO?
WHAT'S HERE? A CUP, CLOSED IN MY TRUE LOVE'S HAND?
POISON, I SEE, HATH BEEN HIS TIMELESS END.
O HAPPY DAGGER! THIS IS THY SHEATH. THERE RUST, AND LET ME DIE.

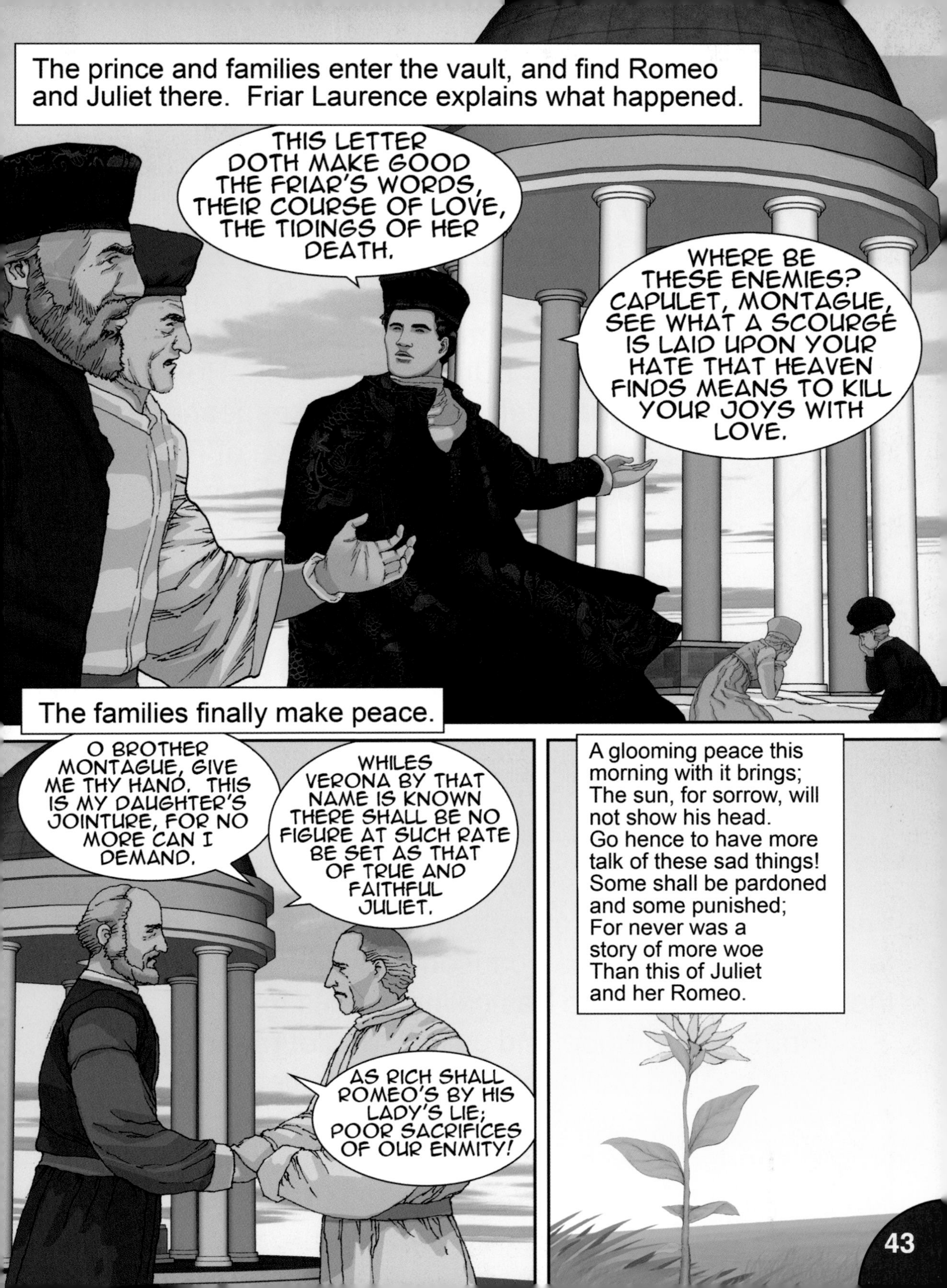
The prince and families enter the vault, and find Romeo and Juliet there. Friar Laurence explains what happened.
THIS LETTER DOTH MAKE GOOD THE FRIAR'S WORDS, THEIR COURSE OF LOVE, THE TIDINGS OF HER DEATH.
WHERE BE THESE ENEMIES? CAPULET, MONTAGUE, SEE WHAT A SCOURGE IS LAID UPON YOUR HATE THAT HEAVEN FINDS MEANS TO KILL YOUR JOYS WITH LOVE.
The families finally make peace.
O BROTHER MONTAGUE, GIVE ME THY HAND. THIS IS MY DAUGHTER'S JOINTURE, FOR NO MORE CAN I DEMAND.
WHILES VERONA BY THAT NAME IS KNOWN THERE SHALL BE NO FIGURE AT SUCH RATE BE SET AS THAT OF TRUE AND FAITHFUL JULIET.
AS RICH SHALL ROMEO'S BY HIS LADY'S LIE; POOR SACRIFICES OF OUR ENMITY!
A glooming peace this morning with it brings; The sun, for sorrow, will not show his head. Go hence to have more talk of these sad things! Some shall be pardoned and some punished; For never was a story of more woe Than this of Juliet and her Romeo.

Behind Romeo and Juliet

William Shakespeare wrote his play *The Most Excellent and Lamentable Tragedy of Romeo and Juliet* between 1594 and 1596. But, the characters Romeo and Juliet were around long before this. Shakespeare based his play on the poem "The Tragicall Historye of Romeus and Juliet" by English poet Arthur Brooke. Brooke had based his poem on an Italian tale by Matteo Bandello. While the characters were well-known, Shakespeare expanded their love story. His version has become one of the most popular plays of all time.

The first authorized printed version of Shakespeare's *Romeo and Juliet* appeared in 1599. In 1623, the collected works of Shakespeare, called the *First Folio*, were printed. Today, the *First Folio* is the source for most of Shakespeare's plays.

Shakespeare sets *Romeo and Juliet* in Verona, Italy. There, the Montague family is feuding with the Capulet family. Their quarrel has caused fighting in the streets of the city, and the Prince has called for this to end.

Romeo Montague and Juliet Capulet meet and fall in love at a masked ball hosted by the Capulets. Because their families are enemies, the two marry in secret. Their time is shortened when Tybalt, a Capulet, seeks out Romeo and challenges him. After Tybalt kills Romeo's friend Mercutio, Romeo kills Tybalt. Romeo is then banished by the Prince of Verona.

Juliet's father does not know that she is married, and he arranges for her to marry the Count Paris. Juliet asks Friar Laurence for help, and they devise a plan to fake her death and have Romeo take her away. Romeo is unaware of the plan, and he kills himself with poison because he thinks Juliet is dead. When Juliet awakes to find her love is dead, she takes her own life with his dagger. The families learn what has happened and end their feud, but it is too late to save their children.

Since it was written, *Romeo and Juliet* has been performed millions of times. In 1599, Shakespeare became part owner of the Globe Theatre in London and his plays were performed there. Today, the characters come to life on stages and in films around the world.

Famous Phrases

Blind is his love.

It is the East and Juliet is the Sun.

My only love sprung from my only hate!

Parting is such sweet sorrow.

What's in a name?

William Shakespeare was baptized on April 26, 1564, in Stratford-upon-Avon, England. At the time, records were not kept of births, however, the churches did record baptisms, weddings, and deaths. So, we know approximately when he was born. Traditionally, his birth is celebrated on April 23.

William was the son of John Shakespeare, a tradesman, and Mary Arden. He most likely attended grammar school and learned to read, write, and speak Latin.

Shakespeare did not go on to the university. Instead, he married Anne Hathaway at age 18. They had three children, Susanna, Hamnet, and Judith. Not much is known about Shakespeare's life at this time. By 1592 he had moved to London, and his name began to appear in the literary world.

In 1594, Shakespeare became an important member of Lord Chamberlain's company of players. This group had the best actors and the best theater, the Globe. For the next 20 years, Shakespeare devoted himself to writing. He died on April 23, 1616, but his works have lived on.

Additional Works by Shakespeare

The Comedy of Errors (1589–94)
The Taming of the Shrew (1590–94)
Romeo and Juliet (1594–96)
A Midsummer Night's Dream (1595–96)
Much Ado About Nothing (1598–99)
As You Like It (1598–1600)
Hamlet (1599–1601)
Twelfth Night (1600–02)
Othello (1603–04)
King Lear (1605–06)
Macbeth (1606–07)
The Tempest (1611)

About the Adapters

Joeming Dunn is a general practice physician and the owner of one of the largest comic companies in Texas, Antarctic Press. He is a graduate of Austin College in Sherman, Texas, and the University of Texas Medical Branch in Galveston. He currently lives in San Antonio.

Dr. Dunn has written or co-authored medical and graphic novel texts. He and his wife, Teresa, have two bright and lovely girls, Ashley and Camerin.

Rod Espinosa has worked in advertising, software entertainment, and film. Today, he lives in San Antonio, Texas, and produces stunning graphic novels including *Dinowars, Neotopia, Metadocs, Battle Girls,* and many others. His graphic novel *Courageous Princess* was nominated for an Eisner Award and *Neotopia* was nominated for the Max und Moritz Award.

Glossary

adieu - a French word for "good-bye."

apothecary - one who sells drugs for medical purposes.

bandy - to toss back and forth.

bite my thumb - to give an insulting gesture.

collier - a person who carries coal. In Shakespeare's time, these people were seen as evil and dirty.

consortest - to keep company with.

dram - a small amount of a drink.

endart mine eye - let my eye shoot Love's darts.

fray - a fight or dispute.

hie - hurry.

shrift - a confession.

shrive - to set free.

soft - wait a moment.

sojourn - a temporary stay.

solemnity - a time-honored tradition.

truckle bed - a bed on rollers that can be stored under a standing bed.

Web Sites

To learn more about William Shakespeare, visit ABDO Publishing Company on the World Wide Web at **www.abdopublishing.com**. Web sites about Shakespeare are featured on our Book Links page. These links are routinely monitored and updated to provide the most current information available.